A GOLD MEDAL MAN

Biography of Kenneth "Tug" Wilson

VANESSA E. CURRY

SPARK Publications
Charlotte, North Carolina

A Gold Medal Man:
Biography of Kenneth "Tug" Wilson
Vanessa E. Curry

Designed, produced, and published by SPARK Publications
SPARKpublications.com
Charlotte, North Carolina

This story is based on "The Tug Wilson Story," an autobiography published in 1967 as part of the book *The Big Ten,* written by Kenneth Leon "Tug" Wilson and Jerry Brondfield. Tug's recollections of specific events and conversations are used in this publication with the consent of Tug's granddaughter, Linda Kellough, acting as a representative of the Wilson family.

Information obtained from the Atwood-Hammond Public Library's special collection of Tug Wilson's memorabilia, including photographs, letters, telegrams, also was used with permission.

Photos also provided by Drake University, University of Illinois; United States Olympic & Paralympic Committee

Background page texture: pingebat/shutterstock.com

Format, July 2022, ISBN: 978-1-953555-29-8
Library of Congress Control Number: 2022911036

DEDICATION

To all lifelong learners and to the town
librarians who do so much to preserve
history that informs and, hopefully,
inspires many generations to come.

CONTENTS

Part 3

Part 4

ACKNOWLEDGMENTS

This book would not have been possible without a series of circumstances and events I thankfully recognized as God's plan to help me accomplish my writing goal. Losing a job during a worldwide pandemic granted me all the time I needed to focus on research and writing without the pressure of normal day-to-day activities.

Special thanks to Linda, Donald, and Tug Kellough for allowing me to reprint information from their grandfather's writing: "The Tug Wilson Story," as part of a much larger publication, *The Big Ten*. Linda's writing contribution gives readers an insight that only someone who knew Tug could provide. It also was a pleasure to listen to Bruce Carroll's stories about growing up with his cousin, Tug.

There were plenty of friends, family, and others who kept me motivated throughout the writing process: Marsha Burgener gave me all the library space I needed, any time I needed it, and access to valuable sources; Marilyn Covey consistently encouraged me; Betty Gomes inspired me with insight and connections; my brother Eric enlightened me with his sports acumen and advice, which helped clear my mind on occasions; and the rest of my family, who resisted the urge to pepper me with the inevitable question, "Are you done yet?" Special thanks to Donna Mills for believing in me and providing much-needed support and to Lori and Gary Kroll, who are always available to lend an ear.

To Maddix Stirrett, Bryleigh and Bentley Brace, and Paul Woolly for reading and providing feedback; Amy Lee for providing old photos of Atwood; Noelle De Atley for introducing me to SPARK Publications and to Fabi Preslar for taking on this project; Kent Brown for his connections and encouragement; and to Yvonne Thrash and Glenna M. who gave me a little kick in the pants for motivation when I needed it.

INTRODUCTION

If you drive east or west along US Highway 36 between
Decatur and Tuscola in central Illinois, you can catch a
glimpse of a little town called Atwood. But don't blink; you
might miss it. With fewer than 1,300 residents, Atwood's
population barely has doubled since it officially came into
existence in 1884. Farming and supporting businesses always
have been a mainstay for the community, but over time its self-
sufficiency gave way to families who worked and spent their
income elsewhere.

The town's claim to fame? Well, Atwood isn't really well
known for anything unless you count the high school football
team winning the state championship in 1980. That
achievement is difficult to publicize since someone stole the
highway sign memorializing that accomplishment. More
notably, the school district no longer exists since residents
voted to be annexed by another in 2013, razing the empty high
school building a year later. If you dig deep enough in the
newspaper clippings and other notes or books kept at the town
library, you can find the name of at least one notable native:
Kenneth Leon "Tug" Wilson, a farm boy whose career path
took him all over the world to promote the benefits of
amateur sports.

Although I grew up in Atwood, I had never heard his name,
not even from my father or my grandparents, who spent a
majority of their lives in the same town. My first peek into
Tug's life came from a spiral-bound book covered with thick,
yellow paper and marked with the awkwardly worded title

Linda Kellough, right, and Katie Riesner, left (Tug's granddaughter and great-granddaughter respectively), unveil the historic marker during an August 21, 2020, dedication ceremony in Atwood.

"Atwood High Alumnus Containing Sketches from the Posts and Memories of Alumnus of 40-50-60-or So Years Ago." The notebook was among several boxes of items I purchased at an auction containing the remaining estate of longtime Atwood jeweler Rex Hadden. The book comprises about 125 typed pages, obviously created on an old manual typewriter. There is no publication date, but it's filled with information I never knew about my hometown and its people. I read the book in one sitting.

Every day is a school day for a lifelong learner like me. I love to read. I love to find the story within a story. I love to follow the thread linking bits of information that draw me deeper into a topic or onto a completely different path. This curiosity, this thirst for information, served me well during my career as a journalist and now as an author. This gift led me to several marvelous stories, just like the one you are about to read.

Tug's biographical information, in particular, caught my attention. An Olympian? Athletics director at Northwestern University? Big Ten commissioner? President of the US Olympic Committee? "Wow!" I thought. Why haven't I heard of this before? I searched (or googled) his name on the internet, which led me to the book, *The Big Ten*, he published with journalist Jerry Brondfield in 1967. I read the autobiography portion titled "The Tug Wilson Story," and the plethora of historic information it provided fascinated me. That fascination led to the formation of a committee that sponsored the Tug Wilson historical marker sanctioned by the Illinois State Historical Society. That marker memorializing his accomplishments now stands in Rajah Memorial Park on Magnolia Avenue in Atwood, about a mile from the farm where Tug grew up.

It also sparked the storyteller in me. Tug's athletic career and his contributions to amateur sports are an inspiring story that needs to be shared. Tug never forgot the small central Illinois town he called home, so recognizing him in return is long overdue.

PART 1:

From Atwood to Antwerp

A plow horse provided entertainment and transportation for the Wilson children, Winifred, Tug, and Henry, in this 1907 photograph.

CHAPTER 1

Life on the Farm

Tug Wilson always assumed he would earn his living as a farmer, cultivating the black central Illinois soil just like his father and his father's father. It's a vocation he learned to appreciate growing up amid the fertile grain fields that sustained generations of families.

He was proud to be a country boy, rising to the sound of his father's call at 4:30 a.m. each day, so he could prepare for morning chores. It would be relatively quiet as the light from Tug's kerosene lamp revealed the worn path from the house to the barn. In the winter, the silence would be broken by the crunching of his boots packing the snow with each step. In the spring, it was the intermittent chirps from early birds calling to one another among the trees. He could hear the horses, cows, and other animals beginning to stir, stretching and shifting their weight as they anticipated his arrival. The daily routine involved feeding and watering the livestock, milking, and collecting eggs twice a day. Remember, too, that farm animals weren't considered family pets. Instead, they were sources of food, a means of travel, or muscle for pulling plows and wagons, all vital to the family's survival.

Tug usually worked up quite an appetite before sitting down to a hearty breakfast. It wasn't uncommon for young Tug to consume three or four eggs, several strips of bacon, a couple of slices of bread, and a large glass of milk before heading off to school or back to work.

On the farm, everyone contributed to the family's well-being—putting food on the table, caring for the livestock, farming, and keeping the home repaired. And there was always something needing to be done: mending fences, chopping wood, repairing equipment, cleaning stalls, oiling the harnesses, filling the grain bins, or stacking hay. Depending on the season, it wasn't uncommon for Tug to miss a few days of school to help plant or harvest the corn or wheat. Hard work didn't bother him, but he sometimes found a way to make it a little more fun. Bare cornstalks became spears to throw as far as he could, and filled grain wagons became chariots ripe for a race back to the barn. Competitions involving his sister and brother were common.

Occasionally, there was time for hunting squirrels and rabbits, fishing or swimming with friends at a nearby stream, or going to town to watch the men play baseball. It was the kind of upbringing that instilled the virtues of responsibility and discipline while building good character and a healthy body. That's the childhood Tug lived and loved—an experience he believed every boy should have.

The Wilson family valued formal education as well. For that, Tug, his sister, and brother attended school in nearby Atwood, a small farming community created when the Indiana and Illinois Central Railroad Company built a route from Indianapolis to Springfield in 1873. The school's well-traveled, college-educated teachers taught more than just reading, writing, and 'rithmetic. They shared their experiences of life in big cities, in other countries, and among different cultures, hoping to expand their students' knowledge beyond the confines of a small town. They also encouraged participation in extracurricular activities, physical and academic, to build a healthy appreciation for competition while encouraging their students to explore their personal interests. In that aspect, teachers seemed to have something in common with farmers. Whether in fields of dirt or receptive young minds, they both sowed seeds in hopes of a bountiful yield.

Tom Samuels certainly wasn't a farmer, but he did plant something important. He was a respected former superintendent and coach at Atwood Township High School who encouraged Tug to train to become an Olympic athlete. At the end of summer in 1912, Samuels[1] gathered the high school boys—all nine of them—to recount incredible stories about watching the Olympic Games in Stockholm, Sweden, while touring Europe that summer. He described how American Jim Thorpe made history by winning gold medals in the pentathlon and decathlon.

"If you start training now, you can make an Olympic team someday," Samuels told the boys.[2]

Tug seemed skeptical. He found it difficult to believe a farm boy like himself from a town with fewer than seven hundred residents could be good enough to compete against some of the best athletes in the world. He asked Samuels how it could be possible.

"How far is your farm from the school?" Samuels asked Tug.

"About a mile," he replied.

"If you run back and forth to school each day, you'll be a great distance man," Samuels told him.

Sixteen-year-old Tug loved sports, and he liked the idea of one day becoming a member of such a team. He followed Samuels's advice and began a running regimen that strengthened his muscles and mind enough to become a competitive high school and collegiate athlete.

---

1 Samuels left Atwood to begin his law career in Decatur, but he apparently returned often to Atwood while courting his former student, Pauline Flickenger, whom he married after she graduated in 1912. She was in the same class as Winifred Wilson, Tug's sister.
2 Wilson, Tug, and Jerry Brondfield. 1967. *The Big Ten*, Prentice Hall, 1967, 101.

Atwood's first school building burned in 1913,
one year before Tug was to graduate.

CHAPTER 2

The Early Years

The Village of Atwood was still in its infancy when Kenneth Leon Wilson was born on March 27, 1896, in his family's white cottage on north Main Street. He was the second of three children born to Charles W. and Nelda Gross Wilson, but no one called him by his formal name. They called him "Little Tug" or "Tug," a nickname he shared with his father. Folks considered Charles Wilson a civic-minded man and an athlete[3] reminiscent of the English fighter Tug Wilson, a bare-knuckled boxer who cunningly completed three rounds with famed heavyweight champion John L. Sullivan in an exhibition match.[4]

The Wilson and Gross families had settled in and around a cluster of small Piatt and Douglas County towns: Hammond, Pierson, Bement, Monticello, Mackville, and Garrett. Nelda's father, Henry Gross, was one of four brothers who emigrated from Germany to settle in Mackville along Lake Fork stream[5] to engage in businesses and trades. The town's population

3 Charles Wilson served on the Atwood school board for nearly eleven years and enjoyed playing baseball.
4 "Sick Sullivan" *The Cleveland Leader* July 19, 1882, 3. Timothy Hughes Rare and Early Newspapers with Wikipedia notes.
5 "Mackville History." Atwood Centennial Book 1873-1973. Area residents consider Lake Fork a river although technically it is a stream.

of 150 depended upon the stream to power the grist and sawmills and to transport trade goods, crops, and people. That all changed when the new rail line came through, providing quicker and more convenient transportation. The route bypassed Mackville and, as a result, the town's population dwindled as residents—including Henry Gross and his family—moved one mile east to a grove of trees near the railroad. Folks initially referred to it as being "at the woods." This new town that straddles the Piatt/Douglas County line was officially incorporated as the Village of Atwood on January 14, 1884.[6] In time, the homes and businesses in Mackville fell to ruin, replaced by fields of corn, wheat, or soybeans. Now, only a cemetery retains the name of the former town.

Tug's parents attended high school in Atwood, although Charles elected to take the county exam for teachers instead of graduating.[7] Nelda was one of the first two students to graduate from Atwood High School in 1887. She married Charles in 1892, and both initially pursued teaching as a career. Tug may not have had that physical training opportunity if his parents hadn't moved to the Wilson family homestead when he was just five years old. The home, located northeast of the Atwood school, was the same one Charles and his sister had lived in with their parents. When Tug was old enough to go to school, he joined his older sister, Winifred, walking to Atwood.

The roads then were just dirt, accustomed to travelers on horseback or in horse-drawn wagons. Most people just walked while trying to avoid dried wagon ruts and kicking up dust during the summer, slipping and sloshing through the mud during the rainy season, and plodding through the snow-covered frozen ground in the winter. In

---

6 Atwood Centennial Book 1873-1973.
7 April 20, 1934, obituary "Charles W. Wilson Died Tuesday" (newspaper not identified, found as clip in Atwood-Hammond library file).

time, younger brother Henry joined his siblings on the daily commute to school. Occasionally they rode horseback, as did many of their classmates, hitching their horses to a post just outside the school—a two-story, wood-framed building set in a grove of box elder trees. The building housed both the grade school and high school. They added another wing years later to accommodate a growing population of students.[8]

This wood-framed building, built in the late 1880s, served as Atwood's first school and housed elementary and high school classrooms. First destroyed the building in 1913

It was an interesting time to grow up in the Midwest. Automobiles, electricity, and even telephones were uncommon. Playing sports, especially baseball, was a popular pastime for boys and men, but country schools rarely had the facilities to accommodate official teams. Even opportunities to watch collegiate or professional athletic competitions were rare, and following America's favorite pastime on the radio wasn't available until the 1920s. Summertime offered the best, and sometimes only, opportunities for athletic competition during Tug's younger years. His father allowed him to go to the weekly town baseball game on Wednesday or Sunday night and, if he was lucky, the older players allowed him and his friends to catch fly balls (called shagging) in the outfield during warmups.

During the summer, county fairs were one of the most anticipated social events. While the crops soaked up the sun or rain, farmers loaded their families into wagons and directed the horses to Monticello, the county seat of Piatt County, or nearby counties, to enjoy livestock shows, farm equipment and new product demonstrations, outrageous attractions, and a multitude of contests involving garden crops, baked goods, sewing, and athleticism. Tug's first ride in an automobile consisted of a trip around the horse track for a twenty-five-cent

---

8 Atwood Centennial Book 1873-1973, school section.

fee during one fair. At another, Tug followed in the footsteps of his namesake, climbing into the ring with an experienced wrestler who entertained fairgoers with his ability to quickly and easily pin his competitor to the mat. Tug's first experience in athletic competition came during a fair before he was even ten years old. He lined up on the dirt horse track with other boys his age for the fifty-yard dash. He won the race but nearly lost his pants. "I got off to a good start but suddenly my suspenders parted from my pants and my pants started south," he recalled. "I finished with one hand clutching them but luckily I had enough of a lead to win."[9] Tug received fifty cents as a prize—a lot more money than the three-cents-a-bushel his father paid him for shucking corn.

9 *The Big Ten,* 102. Tug loved to tell stories about his boyhood. In a similar story told during his retirement party, Tug tells of entering a fifty-yard dash during a Fourth of July celebration in which he split the pants of his only suit. Whether the two similar stories are one in the same (with slightly different outcomes) is unknown.

"Atwood got its name from citizens referring to being 'at the woods.'"

Atwood Centennial Book

Yearbook photo of Atwood's 1912 high school track team.
Tug is standing back row center.

CHAPTER 3

High School

High school finally provided Tug with the opportunity to play organized sports—when there were enough boys to form a team. When Samuels became school superintendent in 1909-1910, there were only thirty-three students in all. Tug, a freshman, was one of nine boys enrolled. On top of that, the school lacked a gymnasium or track, and the school officials could only provide limited equipment or uniforms. One of Tug's first athletic uniforms was made from a pair of cut-down overalls.[10] Atwood seemed an unlikely place for twenty-six-year-old Samuels to begin his career. The University of Illinois law school graduate[11]—often dressed in a three-piece suit with a stiff penny collar—offered a stark contrast to his students' simple, well-worn clothes. Still, Samuels was an avid sports fan and determined to build basketball and track teams under the school's colors of black and orange. That ambition impressed the boys, who Samuels kept busy practicing an hour or more after school from September to June. If Tug also stuck to his running regimen to and from school during those same

---

10 Gordon, Dick. 1955. "Personality of the Week." *Star Tribune* (Minneapolis, Minnesota), July 3, 1955.
11 Petrina, Dave. 1989. "Decatur attorney Thomas Samuels Sr. dies." *Decatur Herald-Review,* May 31, 1989.

months, presumably he ran over one thousand miles during his high school athletic career—the distance from Chicago to Jacksonville, Florida, as the crow flies.

Tug stood out among the group too. At nearly six feet one inch tall, he was about four inches taller than the average American man at the time.[12] Tug was a trim 190 pounds but with muscular legs and arms, and he had large hands. His cropped hair drew attention to his most prominent feature, his ears. His first love was baseball, but school officials struggled to field a team consistently. Instead, Tug focused on track and basketball.

Samuels's devotion to producing better athletes and winning teams included buying new uniforms (with a simple "A" on the chest) and equipment—including a Spaulding brand pole vault, discus, shot (for shot put), and hammer. For other needs, Samuels just made do. Since there was no actual track, practice or meets involved using the middle of a wide dirt road—a venue that sometimes included the north end of Main Street. They used truss benches as hurdles, borrowed from organizers of the Atwood Fall Festival. The only time the team experienced a "track" was at the county meet conducted at the fairground's dirt horse-trotting track. Samuels also instituted the Fall Handicap—an intramural competition he used as a recruiting tool, recognizing talent in the younger classes. His efforts to establish Atwood as a formidable opponent succeeded when Atwood won the Piatt County championship in 1910[13] for the first time. Samuels hoped that title would motivate future teams. Indeed, Atwood won the Douglas-Moultrie County field meet the next year, giving Atwood more bragging rights and another pennant to admire on the schoolhouse wall.

---

12 Johnson, David. 2016. "How Tall Would You Have Been 100 Years Ago?" Time.com, July 27, 2016.
13 *The Post*, student yearbook at Atwood High School, 1910-1916.

Tug played a small role in the team's success his freshman year, but fans and coaches[14] quickly realized his athleticism. He impressed them with the way he challenged himself, always working to improve his performance, and he wasn't afraid to try a new technique either. "Kenneth is not only the wonder of his class, but he is one of the wonders of the track team," a classmate wrote in the 1911 edition of *The Post*, the school's yearbook.

A drawing in the 1912 edition of the *The Post* used to illustrate a story about Tug's athletic accomplishments

Wilson the Sophomore Basket Ball Star.

Throughout high school, Tug participated in running and jumping events, although throwing weights—especially the hammer—became his specialty. The hammer thrown in this sport isn't like the hammer used to pound nails. A sporting hammer consists of a sixteen-pound metal ball attached to a steel wire with a handle at the other end. The athlete grabs the handle, swings his body around and then releases it, flinging the ball and wire as far as he can. At first, Tug practiced throwing a twelve-pound sledgehammer. When the school acquired an official hammer, Tug took it home and practiced throwing in a cow pasture. At the beginning of his junior year, Tug already held a school record of throwing 140 feet, 6 inches. "Wilson has won a name for himself

---

14 During high school, Tug played for a succession of coaches: Samuels, J. W. Madden, and Arthur W. Niedermeyer.

among high schools of central Illinois and if he keeps on training, he will probably become famous as a college athlete," another classmate noted.[15]

During his junior and senior years, Tug led his team not only as its captain but in scoring points, often placing in the top two in running, jumping, and throwing events. In 1913, he won first place at the Piatt County Meet in high jump and hammer throw and third place in hammer at the Central Illinois Interscholastic Meet. As a senior, Tug scored twenty-three of the team's fifty-five total points at one meet,[16] with four first-, one second-, and one third-place finishes.

Basketball (or in the beginning: "basket ball") became a regular sport for boys in Atwood when the Piatt County Athletic Association adopted it as a sport in 1912. None of the students who formed the first Atwood team had ever played the game, but they quickly learned. Tug played center and served as team captain his senior year, all while earning praise for his shooting and ball-handling abilities. "He is said to be the best center in the county on account of the many games won solely by his impetuous rush and skill as a goal shooting," a classmate wrote in *The Post*. "He has always been the bulwark of the team." In fact, Tug contended he once scored fifty-three points in a game against neighboring Cerro Gordo.[17]

Playing basketball in Atwood was a challenge because the school lacked a gymnasium. During Tug's high school years, the team played on a dirt court outdoors and often contended with strong wind, extreme temperatures, and even snow. When the weather was unbearable, the team played at the downtown Opera House, located in the Modern Woodmen of America building, a venue that offered an unorthodox playing strategy. One bizarre play consisted of disappearing through one stage door and reappearing through another—confusing the defender, Tug later recalled.

---

15 *The Post*, 1913.
16 *The Post*, 1914.
17 Schrader, Bill. 1961. *Champaign News Gazette*, May 14, 1961.

Collection of high school track meet ribbons donated to the Atwood-Hammond Public Library by Tug's grandchildren

When he wasn't playing for the school's basketball or track teams, Tug played on the town's baseball team—often traveling in a horse-drawn wagon ten miles or more to play a Sunday-evening game.

Tug also had other interests: acting parts in school plays, serving as the business manager for the school yearbook, and public speaking. As a member of the Alpha Literary Society, Tug studied and practiced the art of extempore speaking—a skill that proved valuable later during his professional career. He also maintained good grades, earning high marks in English, German, history, and economics. Tug struggled a little with physics[18] during his senior year. He graduated in 1914—the only boy in a class of seven[19]—with the plan to pursue a college degree. According to his class prophecy, "after a few years' experience in teaching, he expects to specialize in agriculture in order to take his place with the progressive farmers of the present age."

18 Comes from a report card saved by Tug Wilson and included in memorabilia donated to the Atwood-Hammond Public Library.
19 Tug's class was also known as the "only sheep shed grads." The summer before his senior year, fire destroyed the Atwood school. A temporary building known as the sheep shed was used while a new school building was constructed.

Atwood Main Street looking south, early 1900s

CHAPTER 4

A Taste of Teaching

Tug's parents, both college educated, always encouraged their children to pursue a college degree. After teaching a few terms, Charles attended UIC College of Pharmacy at the University of Illinois Chicago and returned to work with Dr. James Abrams in an Atwood drugstore for many years while also farming. Nelda attended Valparaiso University in Indiana for a few terms before taking a teaching position at a county school.

Tug didn't lack the desire to attend college; he just couldn't afford it. So he turned to teaching to earn his way, just as his parents and older sister[20] had done. Tug took the teacher certification exam when he was seventeen years old but failed. The county school superintendent gave him a second chance. If Tug completed six hours of summer school at the University of Illinois, the superintendent would pass him. Off Tug went to the University of Illinois Urbana-Champaign, enrolling in an English class for a two-hour credit and in the school's first summer coaching program for the remaining credits. Athletics director George Huff promoted the coaching school to fill a growing need for high school and college coaches.

---

20 Winifred Wilson graduated from the University of Illinois and taught school in Atwood.

The idea of formal training in sports and coaching intrigued Tug, who successfully passed all his classes. Armed with his teaching certificate, Tug didn't have to look far for a job. In addition to several established "town schools," nearly a dozen rural schools called Piatt or Douglas Counties home. There were no school buses in those days, so families living too far from town often joined forces to create their own schools. Shonkwiler, Meeker, Easton, Landis, Harshbarger, and Coffin were just a few of these country schools named after the family who created them. Officials at the Harshbarger School—a small framed building heated by a hand-fired stove—offered Tug a job for $75 a month. As the only teacher, Tug taught forty-eight students in eight grades.

Tug came to the job highly recommended by his former Atwood coach and teachers who described him as an industrious, responsible, intelligent leader "well fitted" for teaching.[21] Still, Tug wasn't too sure about grading papers and planning programs. He understood what it was like to be a country boy who sometimes needed to miss class to plant crops or to shuck corn. As a teacher, however, Tug needed to keep his students motivated to learn. Forming athletic teams to compete with four nearby county schools proved a popular decision among the boys and girls who were so enthusiastic about competing; they often arrived at school at 7 a.m. to practice before class. They played basketball on a crude outdoor dirt court, competing in running events and even a one-mile bicycle race. "All the kids loved it and a lot of farm chores went unattended, but if this was the only way I could keep kids interested in school, I was willing to face up to the ire of a lot of farmer-fathers," Tug said.[22]

---

21 Anna Stansbury, who taught Latin and German, Principal Lottie Cook, and Superintendent Arthur W. Niedermeyer each wrote a letter of recommendation. The letters are part of a collection of material donated to the Atwood-Hammond Public Library.
22 *The Big Ten*, 110.

Tug (holding basketball) taught at Harshbarger School in 1915.

If he wasn't needed on his father's farm, Tug continued playing baseball after school and during the summer on a team comprising former high school players and other young men. It kept him in shape.

After two years of teaching, the twenty-year-old Tug decided it was time to go back to school. He took his savings of nearly $800 and enrolled at the University of Illinois as an agriculture major. "I figured that when I'd acquired some modern ideas about farming, I'd go back to take over the family acreage and turn it into a profitable venture," Tug said.[23]

He left home one day in September 1916 during a downpour. Driving the family car to Champaign was out of the question since the rain had turned the dirt roads into rivers of mud. So his father hitched up the mule team and plodded ten miles east to the Tuscola station to catch the passenger train going north. The trip took hours, but gave Charles time for a heartfelt conversation with his oldest son. Just before the train pulled out of the station, Charles gave his son a checkbook and encouraged him to use it if he ever needed it. "The confidence he had in me was enough for me to make a silent promise never to let him down," Tug said.[24]

---

23 *The Big Ten,* 117.
24 *The Big Ten,* 117.

Tug as an Illini football player

CHAPTER 5

College Athlete or Soldier?

Although Champaign-Urbana was only thirty-five miles northeast of Atwood, it was the farthest distance from his farm that Tug had ever been; it was also the largest city he had ever seen at this point in his life. In 1916, nearly three times more people lived in the twin cities than the combined populations of Atwood, Hammond, Pierson, Garrett, Bement, and Monticello.

Champaign, like Atwood, was settled because of the railroad. The Illinois Central Railroad created its Chicago to Mobile, Alabama, route in 1855,[25] passing two miles west of Urbana. The one-and-a-half-mile gap of land—mostly muddy fields—between the two cities became a college campus when Illinois Industrial University opened in 1868 with about fifty students. The school later changed its name to the University of Illinois to reflect a more diverse curriculum. When Tug arrived on campus, university enrollment—around six thousand students—was nearly ten times the population of Atwood, but that fact didn't intimidate Tug, who embraced the opportunity to broaden his horizons.

He didn't waste any time immersing himself in his new environment. Just off the train, Tug lugged his belongings

---

25 Champaignil.gov (accessed 2021).

toward campus, found lodging in a rooming house, and then registered in the College of Agriculture. The next day he showed up for freshman football tryouts—a sport Tug had never played. Atwood initially rejected football,[26] considering it too dangerous after two boys in a neighboring community died playing a game. The hardened-leather helmet with protective earflaps and padding wasn't a common part of the football uniform until the 1920s. Atwood fielded its first team one year after Tug graduated.[27] Tug's knowledge of the game consisted of attending one game in which he watched Illinois quarterback, Potsy Clark, clinch a home-game win against Chicago with a spectacular run.

During the first day of practice, coach Ralph Jones sized up Tug and directed him onto the field.

"Take the right tackle position and run through some plays," he told Tug.[28]

"What is a right tackle and where do I stand?" Tug asked with a hint of embarrassment.

Tug learned the basics of the game within two months and played in enough games to earn "his numerals" that first year. Although clearly not an outstanding player, Tug's dedication, enthusiasm, and toughness kept him a part of the Fighting Illini or "The Tribe"[29]—an athletic program that produced Illinois greats such as George Halas (who later founded the Chicago Bears professional football team), legendary coach

---

26 According to the *Washington Post*, "How Teddy Roosevelt Helped Save Football," by Katie Zezima, May, 29 2014, forty-five people died playing football in America between 1900 and 1905.

27 Atwood player Carl Harshbarger died in 1920, five weeks after being injured in a game between Atwood and Tuscola. He is buried in the Mackville Cemetery. "Football Game Cause of Death: Carl Harshbarger of Atwood Succumbs in Decatur Hospital." November 19, 1920, 3.

28 *The Big Ten*, 117.

29 The University of Illinois didn't adopt Chief Illiniwek as its mascot or symbol until 1926. It was retired in 2007 under pressure from Native American organizations. "Defiant Until the End." *Chicago Tribune*, February 22, 2007, chicagotribune.com.

Robert "Bob" Zuppke, and athletics director George Huff. "The Tribe" won a national football title in 1919.

As soon as football season ended, Tug turned to basketball under Coach Zuppke, who recognized Tug's talent and anticipated his return to the court his sophomore year as a varsity starter. Tug's first bad break of his athletic career came near the end of basketball season when he fractured his left wrist while attempting a rebound.

Eight weeks in a cast didn't help as the injury left his hand stiff and bent like a claw. Huff sent Tug and two other athletes[30] to see John "Bonesetter" Reese in Youngstown, Ohio. Reese wasn't a doctor, but a mill worker trained in manipulating muscle strains and tendons.[31] Although he generally focused on helping coworkers, Reese earned a reputation among athletes—initially baseball players—for relieving their pain and returning them to work. Medical professionals doubted his abilities, but people in some circles considered Reese a miracle worker.

Tug appeared apprehensive as he entered Reese's office, where a skeleton dangled on a wall covered with pictures of human anatomy. Reese examined Tug carefully.

"Son, this going to hurt," Reese finally said as he placed Tug's wrist on a table.[32]

Reese didn't lie. Breaking all the adhesions that had formed on Tug's wrist was a painful experience, but it worked. His wounds eventually healed, and he regained full flexibility of his hand and wrist.

As predicted, Tug made the varsity basketball team as a center his sophomore year but suffered another injury mid-season. He had torn the semilunar cartilage in his knee, an injury that could have ended his athletic career. The injury,

---

30 Swede Rundquist, captain of the football team, and George Halas also went to Ohio for treatment. *The Big Ten*, 118.
31 https://sabr.org/bioproj/person/bonesetter-reese/.
32 *The Big Ten*, 118.

better known as a torn meniscus, occurs when the knee is forcefully twisted or rotated. Repairing the cartilage required expensive surgery that had yet to become common treatment. After consulting with his father, Tug underwent surgery,[33] which left him in a heavy cast from his hip to his ankle for months. He couldn't finish that season but returned to play his final two years.

The rangy center controlled the ball well on offense and defensively often broke up the opponent's play. It wasn't unusual for Tug to lead his team in scoring, either. During his junior year, Tug scored six field goals and five free throws in the 25–15 win over Wisconsin.[34] He scored one hundred points that season.[35] They appointed Tug as team captain his senior year, although he lost his starting position to sophomore standout Chuck Carney.[36] He accepted the change like a true sportsman, but watching the game from the bench admittedly was disappointing. "The only thing that gave me any solace was the fact that Carney immediately was recognized as the finest basketball player Illinois ever had," Tug said. "I was happy to get in enough games to make my letter."[37]

After basketball came outdoor track season. Tug stuck with the weights—shot put, discus, hammer, and the javelin. Tug, while still in his leg cast, was introduced to the latter sport his sophomore year when it made its debut during a meet between Illinois and the University of Notre Dame. As he watched other athletes attempt to throw the spear-like instrument, Tug bragged to his friends he could do better. "I

---

33 Tug recalled a Dr. Porter (no first name found) performed the rare operation in Chicago with an audience of two hundred doctors and surgeons observing. *The Big Ten*, 118.
34 *The Illio*, the student yearbook at the University of Illinois, 1920, 262.
35 *The Illio*, 1920, 264.
36 The only University of Illinois athlete and the first conference athlete to make all-American in both football and basketball. https://fightingillini.com/honors/hall-of-fame/chuck-carney/15.
37 *The Big Ten*, 137–138.

Tug throwing a javelin during his collegiate
career at the University of Illinois

think I could toss that thing farther than those guys even with
this cast on my leg," he said.[38]

Tug picked up a javelin, hobbled a few steps, cocked his
arm over his shoulder and heaved it just as he had done with
cornstalks back on the farm. The javelin flew downfield toward
two coaches. "Watch out!" Tug and his friends shouted in
unison. One coach turned just as the steel-tipped javelin flew
within inches of his head. That coach was Knute Rockne, the
legendary Notre Dame coach. He stormed over to Tug. "Are
you an idiot?" he asked.[39]

On top of that, Rockne didn't believe Tug had thrown
the javelin that far. "So, I threw it again—even farther," Tug
recalled. Rockne's demeanor changed immediately, politely

---

38 *The Big Ten,* 125.
39 White, Maury. 1979. *The Des Moines Register,* February 6, 1979, Maury
White column.

asking to "borrow" Tug to throw for the Fighting Irish the next weekend.[40] Even with a cast on his leg, Tug won every dual meet javelin throw for the rest of the season. At the Big Ten Conference championships in Chicago, Tug threw it 177 feet, 2¼ inches[41] to claim his first title in the sport. He was named to the all-American track team.

Tug also claimed a gold medal in a one-time competition he aced, the hand grenade throw. The unorthodox event had become a popular addition to collegiate meets to prepare those who might serve in World War I. The contest required the athlete to throw an unfused grenade at a bull's-eye target. Tug hit dead center five out of five throws, earning him accolades as "a good soldier."[42]

As a junior, Tug repeated his championship javelin performance with a throw of 163 feet, 11½-inches and finished second in the hammer throw.[43] His senior year, he finished second in the javelin and third in both the hammer and discus.[44]

Tug considered training under track coach Harry Gill as a tremendous experience. A tall, lanky Canadian, Gill had been a multi-event athlete at the Harvard School of Physical Training and had once held the world record in the discus. He was in the middle of his coaching career at Illinois when Tug became part of his team, which won its first Big Ten championship in 1920.

Gill, who looked more like a businessman than a coach,[45] wasn't much of a talker. But like Tug, he was a thinker, always searching for ways to improve performance. The coach decided

---

40 In the early years of collegiate sports, it was not uncommon for athletes from one school to play for another, especially in a different sport. These athletes were considered "tramp athletes."

41 *The Illio*, 1920, 251.

42 *The Illio*, 1920, 257.

43 *Champaign News Gazette*. 1961. May 14, 1961. An article about the same meet in *The Lincoln Star*, "Michigan First in Big Ten Meet," June 8, 1919, page 7, listed the throw at 154 feet, 4 inches.

44 *Decatur Herald and Review*. 1920. June 6, 1920, 9.

45 In 1918, Gill founded Gill Athletics, a company that manufactured athletic equipment, including a javelin made from ash wood. The company, which still exists today in Champaign, Illinois, became a force in many equipment innovations in track and field.

wooden javelins could be improved if they were made of hickory instead of spruce.

"I need a stick of well-seasoned hickory," Gill told Tug one day. "Do you have any rail fences on your farm?"

"Sure, we have the fences," Tug replied.[46]

They drove to the Atwood farm and selected several weathered hickory rails. Gill took the rails to his workshop, trimmed and shaped a rail with sandpaper and a hand lathe according to specific measurements. The javelin Gill made played a crucial role in Tug's "crazy dream" of being an Olympic athlete.

Call of Duty?

The years 1917 and 1918 proved to be challenging in other ways. The United States joined the Allied powers at war in 1917. Up to one thousand students left the University of Illinois to help tend to family farms or join the military.[47] Tug wanted to answer the call too but was turned away from Officer Training School because of his previous knee injury. The Air Force rejected him for poor eyesight. So it was back to college for Tug who, a year later, found himself amidst an influenza pandemic that infected an estimated 2,500 students, caused nineteen student deaths and forced cancellation of some sporting events.[48]

No doubt, sports had become a major part of Tug's daily life. The letters he sent to his parents detailed his experiences, but he didn't tell them he was considering the possibility that athletics, not farming, would become his occupation. He may not have realized it at the time, but his studies and other campus activities also played an important role in preparing him for a forty-five-year career in amateur sports.

---

46 *The Big Ten*, 127.
47 Another three thousand students enrolled in the Student Army Training Corp. "Student Life and Culture Archive," archives.library.illinois.edu.
48 "1918: The Year Without a Homecoming," storied.illinois.edu.

Tug considered Illinois a very friendly university and enjoyed making friends across all disciplines and interests. His accomplishments on the field and court during his freshmen year fueled invitations to rush several fraternities. He decided upon Delta Upsilon, a non-secret, non-hazing[49] fraternity with a mission to build better men. The membership did wonders for Tug's social education. "I know that I owe a great deal more to my fraternity that I can ever pay back," he said. "They knocked a lot of the rough, rural edges off me, kept me at my studies and gave me a lot of encouragement when the going was tough."[50]

In his junior year, Tug was elected president of the Student Union largely because of his campaigning efforts to gain the vote of everyday students rather than appealing to just the fraternity-sorority aligned parties. As president, Tug was called upon to de-escalate a hazing incident between the freshman and sophomore classes, and he reorganized campus dances, making them financially sustainable. In fact, under Tug's leadership, the Student Union ended the year with a surplus of $4,000—funds used to renovate the Union Building. Tug represented the male students at the rededication ceremony where he met the females' representative, Dorothy Shade, the junior class president. Tug's social life improved a great deal after their meeting.

His presidential duties also allowed Tug to form friendships with members of the faculty and administration, relationships that benefited his professional career. As for his studies, Tug continued pursing a degree in agriculture but realized he had taken so many courses in public speaking that he was in danger of not graduating on schedule. He took summer courses to catch up on his degree requirements. Still, Tug developed an

---

49 Tug also was a member of the Ku Klux Klan, an interfraternal society with a pension for alcohol. A report title Ku Klux Klan from the University Archives staff published October 15, 2012, found no direct connection with the controversial national KKK or that the campus society engaged in any racist activity. The Illinois organization changed its name to Tu Mas in 1923.
50 *The Big Ten*, 123.

excellent reputation for speaking and used his persuasiveness to argue for the reinstatement of the football team's star fullback, Jack Crangle, who had been declared ineligible to play.[51]

One of the Greatest Thrills

Anticipation of the 1920 Olympics was at fever pitch, considering World War I forced athletic officials to cancel the 1916 games. Tug nursed the thought of making the US. team as a javelin thrower, but he needed to find a way to get to the Olympic tryouts at Harvard Stadium in Boston. He knew he couldn't afford to pay his own way, and in those days, few universities paid for the transportation of their athletes. Fortunately, he received an invitation from Martin Delaney, athletic director of the Chicago Athletic Club, who wanted to sponsor him and a handful of other athletes. At the end of the spring semester, Tug moved to Chicago, where he lived at the club and trained under Delaney in the discus and javelin. Confident he would make the Olympic team, Tug acquired his passport before leaving for Boston. But fate wasn't so sure. The day before the trials, Tug was stunned to learn the international rules had changed the throwing style for the javelin. He had learned to throw by holding the javelin near its end. The Amateur Athletic Union now required the thrower to grasp it in the middle. Just as Tug familiarized himself with the new hold, trial officials questioned his use of the homemade hickory javelin. Officials wanted it thrown out, but Delaney convinced them it met all specifications. Finally, Tug was cleared to throw.

A javelin competition generally consists of three throws, with each participant throwing once in each round. The participant gains momentum for the throw by running on a short track that ends in a curved arc. The athlete must throw

---

51 Crangle had failed a class but Tug successfully argued that poor advisement assigned him to a course without first taking the prerequisite. Crangle was reinstated.

the javelin overhand without his feet touching the curved arc known as the toe board. This technique often leaves the thrower bouncing on one foot in an attempt to maintain his balance and remain inside the designated area. The javelin must land point first within a designated sector. Officials then measure from the tip of the arc to the landing point. The competitor's longest throw is then compared to those of others to determine a winner.

Tug was so anxious that he fouled on his first throw when he stepped over the toe board. His second throw was quite short. He heard his named called for his third and final throw. "This was it," he thought to himself.[52] A lot of thoughts were going through his mind as he stepped forward. He thought of his family and the hopes they had for him. He thought about Gill and Delaney and their efforts to coach and train him. He even thought about the hickory fence post taken from his farm. Tug grabbed the javelin, took off down the runway, and then let it fly, sticking it 172.44 feet away.[53] The judges didn't have to say a word. "I knew I'd made the Olympic team," Tug said. "It was one of the greatest thrills in my career in sports."[54] Indeed, Tug made the team with the third best overall throw of the competition.

Tug had little time to celebrate making the Olympic team. The day after his successful throw, he and his teammates left Boston and headed to Travers Island in New York, where they would train until July before leaving for Belgium.

---

52 *The Big Ten*, 140.
53 Trackfield.brinkster.net.
54 *The Big Ten*, 140.

"I knew I'd made
the Olympic team.
It was one of the
greatest thrills in my
career in sports."

Tug Wilson

The USS *Princess Matoika*, originally a German
vessel named Princess Alice, was captured
by Americans in 1917, converted to a troop
transport ship, and renamed. (US Navy Photo)

CHAPTER 6

On to Antwerp

Before World War I, Belgium was a growing economic power, with Antwerp—located along the English Channel—being one of its biggest cities and most important trading ports. During the war, the country remained neutral but was invaded and occupied by German forces from 1914 to 1918. The invaders destroyed entire towns, burned universities, massacred thousands of its citizens, and imprisoned or deported thousands of others.

The war forced the International Olympic Committee to cancel the games in 1916, but two years later its members were eager to resume the competition. They chose Antwerp as the site of the Games of the VII Olympiad, hoping to boost morale within the war-ravaged country. They finalized the decision on April 5, 1919, giving Antwerp only sixteen months to prepare—the shortest time period of any Olympic game.

The road to Antwerp for American athletes was paved with water—the Atlantic Ocean. They couldn't fly across it because transatlantic passenger service didn't exist until 1939. They needed a ship, which was scarce in the postwar era, since officials had pressed most passenger vessels into military service. The American Olympic Committee (AOC)[55] turned to the US Navy and US Army for help.

Military officials offered two ships;[56] one of them was the USS *Princess Matoika*, a former German vessel named *Princess Alice* until Americans captured her in 1917, later converting her for troop transport and changing her name. By 1920, the *Matoika*—another name for the famous American Indian Pocahontas—didn't appear like a princess at all. It was old, slow, and rusty.

The AOC coordinators housed Tug and his teammates on a military base while the athletes waited for their ride overseas. That day finally came on July 26, 1920. American Olympic Committee Chairman Gustavus T. Kirby[57] presided over a farewell reception conducted at the Manhattan Opera House. He read congratulatory telegraphs to the team from governors in eleven states before wishing the athletes a good trip and winning performances. The athletes, dressed in navy blue trousers with matching jackets and straw hats, then marched from downtown Manhattan to the Hudson Pier and boarded a ferry to Hoboken, New Jersey.

It was a whirlwind visit to New York City for Tug, who had little experience traveling to big cities. He hadn't visited Chicago in his home state until he was in college. Now he was about to depart for an overseas experience he had dreamed about for eight years. The *Matoika* and the USS *Frederick* awaited the athletes in New Jersey. The latter ship would carry 101 civilians and US Navy-affiliated team members. Tug joined about 230 civilians and US Army-affiliated team members boarding the *Matoika*, which had just unloaded

---

55 The AOC, formed in 1921, was renamed the United States of America Sports Federation in 1940 and again in 1945 to United States Olympic Association. It is now known as the United States Olympic & Paralympic Committee.

56 One of the original ships was deemed unseaworthy and replaced by the *Matoika*.

57 Kirby died March 28, 1956, the year Tug attended his first Olympic Games as president of the United States Olympic Committee.

hundreds of flag-draped coffins carrying the remains of soldiers being returned for burial in American soil. Atwood had lost one of its own during the war. James W. Reeder, 19, died on November 11, 1918[58]—the same day Germany formally surrendered. His remains, however, were not returned until 1921.

It was an ominous beginning to a voyage the athletes wished they could forget. Although the ship had been touted as having "comfortable accommodations,"[59] many of its male athlete passengers soon learned the conditions were hardly bearable. "Everything was in a terrible state of confusion," Tug later wrote.[60] The pungent smell of formaldehyde, decay, and disinfectant permeated the entire ship. The conditions weren't that bad for female athletes, the AOC, and US Army athletes who had been assigned first-class cabins on the upper portion of the ship. The rest, however, were assigned to sleep in hammocks strung up in the former troop quarters below in sweltering heat. It also was infested with the largest rats Tug had ever seen. After two days of rough seas, a group of seasick athletes had to be moved to the sick bay. The limited food available was terrible. Tug said the eating facilities were so poor the team ate in shifts regulated alphabetically. "I was always on the last shift and there wasn't always an abundance of food," he said.[61]

Rough seas and the lack of adequate space also hampered the athletes' attempts to train and contributed to several injuries. But they made do with what they had. They created swimming tanks out of canvas. Javelins were tethered to ropes so they could be thrown overboard and retrieved. The athletes did their best, but the conditions were depressing.

58 Reeder is buried in Mackville Cemetery. American Legion Post 770 in Atwood is named in his honor.
59 "Matoika to Carry American Athletes." New York Times, July 10, 1920, 12, timesmachine.nytimes.com.
60 The Big Ten, 140.
61 The Big Ten, 140.

As the ship neared Antwerp, the dissension came to a head. Shot putter Pat McDonald and swimmer Norman Ross led a group of disgruntled athletes in writing a resolution condemning the AOC for providing unlivable conditions. The group threatened to boycott the Olympic Games if they didn't receive better accommodations in Antwerp as well as on the way home. Tug joined 150 athletes in signing the resolution and sending copies to the US Secretary of War, AOC members, and various members of the press. The grievance received wide coverage in American newspapers—even the *New York Times* wrote about it. The incident eventually became known as the "Mutiny of the *Matoika*."[62]

The voyage to Antwerp was supposed to take eight days, but it wasn't until a rainy August 7— nearly thirteen days later— that the *Matoika* came within sight of Belgium's shores. To make matters worse, the athletes remained on board another day while Olympic organizers attempted to find them a place to stay. The male athletes soon learned city schools would provide them accommodations, but they were not much better than what they had on the ship. Staying in classrooms, the athletes slept on fold-out cots and hard benches with blankets and hay-filled pillows. They also complained of the lack of privacy and hot showers. The athletes again threatened to withdraw from the games but were persuaded once again to change their minds "in the spirit of sportsmanship and of making the best of things."[63]

---

62 A term coined by sportswriter John Kieran in 1936 in his book *The Story of the Olympic Games: 776 B.C. to 1968.*
63 Olympische Spelen–Antwerp 1920, Openingscermonie translated via Google translate.

"Everything was in a terrible state of confusion. The pungent smell of formaldehyde, decay, and disinfectant permeated the entire ship."

Tug Wilson

Opening ceremonies of the 1920 Olympic Games in Antwerp, Belgium

CHAPTER 7

Games of the VII Olympiad

It was a tough assignment to prepare Antwerp for the Olympics. The city was still "licking the wounds of the past war violence" and public interest seemed limited. "Ordinary residents were not interested . . . [they] had other concerns than attending this mundane spectacle," according to one final report.[64] Preparations included removing tons of rubble created by invading armies during the war and building new facilities to accommodate 156 sporting events. With little funding, Belgium officials created seventeen venues using existing facilities, some of which were located outside of Antwerp. Military camps, existing tennis clubs, parks, and even the Antwerp Zoo were used.

Other than actual competition, one of the most exciting events for Olympic athletes is taking part in the opening ceremonies—a custom now known for its spectacular choreographed performances in art, music, dance, and special effects. The games in Antwerp had none of that modern-day pageantry, but for three consecutive Sundays in August, organizers presented a parade on the brick streets through the city. Lines of Antwerp residents and visitors stood four or five

---

64 Olympische Spelen–Antwerp 1920. Openingscermonie translated from Finnish to English via Google translate.

rows deep along the sidewalks while others viewed the festivities from balconies or nearby buildings. Most, however, could not afford the high entrance fees charged at the main stadium—a factor in lower-than-expected attendance.[65]

The Olympics officially opened on August 14, 1920. The day began with a religious service in the Antwerp cathedral that included the congregation singing "De Profundis"—the common name for the 130th Psalm[66]—in honor of those athletes who died during the war. In the afternoon, King Albert I and the royal family arrived at Olympisch Stadion, also known as Kielstadion, then the public procession of delegates began. The stadium, which still needed some finishing touches, comprised an oval dirt track with a grass infield surrounded by covered seating for spectators on both sides. The ends of the stadium consisted of a row of connecting Greek-style pillars leading to a brick clock tower featuring an arched doorway.

During the traditional parade of athletes, Tug joined 288 American athletes[67]—including the first female athletes to compete at the Olympics—marching behind a placard imprinted with the words "United States." Athletes, distinguished by their matching uniforms and their own country's sign, marched in groups into the stadium, which was filled with nearly 2,600 competitors.[68] Sadly, war[69] and a Spanish flu pandemic had claimed the lives of many elite athletes. And athletes from Germany, Austria, Hungary, Bulgaria, Turkey, and the Ottoman Empire had not been invited because they were part of the Central Powers who lost the war. The Soviet Union also did not participate.[70]

---

65 Olympische Spelen–Antwerp 1920. Openingsceremonie.
66 The song begins, "Out of the depths I cry to you O Lord, hear my voice." learnreligions.com.
67 Wikipedia.com.
68 The number included about sixty-five women athletes, including fourteen Americans. En.wikipedia.com.
69 At least 144 Olympians are known to have been killed during WWI, with nearly 55 percent of those from Great Britain or France. US Olympians William Jones Lyshon, a wrester, and Arthur Wear, a tennis player, were among those killed during WWI. Wikipedia.com
70 The Soviets initially renounced competitive sports because they considered it a tool of capitalism.

Nevertheless, the path of participating athletes brought the parade through the arched entrance, around the track, and past the royal stand where they removed their hats in salute to Belgium King Albert I before assembling in the grassy field. The delegates listened as a representative recited the athlete's oath before two hundred Swedish singers, accompanied by Theban[71] trumpets, performed the national song. Flemish singers greeted the athletes with "Too Far and Wide," before cannon shots reverberated throughout the stadium and a flock of doves were released from a basket to fly over the stadium.[72]

For Tug, the moment was a dream come true and a personal highlight of his life. He may not have realized it then, but he became a part of three important firsts in Olympic history: the introduction of the Olympic flag with five interlocking rings symbolizing the unity between five world continents; the release of doves to symbolize peace; and creation of the Olympic oath, "We swear that we will take part in the Olympic Games in a spirit of chivalry, for the honor of our country and for the glory of the sport."

The javelin throw competition occurred on Saturday, the day after the opening ceremony. The event involved twenty-five athletes from twelve different nations. But as Tug watched the preliminary rounds, he soon realized he was "completely outclassed"[73] by throwers from Finland and Sweden. He had thrown his personal best, 52.56 meters (172.44 feet), to make the US Olympic team, but that wouldn't even come close to being in the top ten in Antwerp. The Finns swept the event, winning the bronze, silver, and gold medals. Jonni Myyrä from Finland finished first, setting an Olympic record with a throw of 65.78 meters (215.81 feet).[74]

Tug had five days between the javelin throw and the discus competition. He practiced during those days, but also spent time

---

71 Refers to the city of Thebes in Greece. En.wikipedia.com.
72 Details of the opening ceremony came from Olympische Spelen-Antwerp 1920, openingsceremonie. The report is written in Flemish and was translated through Google translate.
73 *The Big Ten*, 143.
74 Olympics.com.

observing other athletes and watching other competitions. Swimming and track and field events always had been popular, but in 1920 at least eight new sporting competitions were added: archery, boxing, field hockey, weightlifting, polo, rugby union, figure skating, and ice hockey. The Antwerp Games also would be the last time tug-of-war was an official Olympic sport. Tug and a teammate took quite an interest in watching Yale University boxer Eddie Eagan win a gold medal in the light-heavyweight division.

The two-day discus event involved seventeen throwers from eight nations. Tug threw his personal best of 37.58 meters (123.29 feet), enough for tenth place. The Finns took the gold and silver with throws over 44 meters (146 feet), but American Gus Pope[75] claimed the bronze medal with a throw of 42.13 meters (138 feet).[76]

In the end, American athletes won ninety-five medals, including forty-one golds, to claim the overall Olympic victory. For Tug, going home without an Olympic medal wasn't necessarily a disappointment. He couldn't help but think about how taking his former superintendent's advice had led him to compete in the Olympics, a "thrilling experience" even if he didn't win. He was immensely satisfied with earning a spot on the American team and then competing among the best athletes in the world. As Pierre de Coubertin, the father of the modern Olympic Games, once said, "The important thing in life is not the triumph but the struggle; the essential thing is not to have conquered but to have fought well."

Tug wrote Samuels a letter from Antwerp, recalling everything he had seen and done. He ended the letter with an expression of deep gratitude, thanking Samuels for planting the seed that started his athletic career.

---

75 A year after the Olympics, Pope, who competed for the University of Washington, won the 1921 NCAA championships in the shot put and discus, earning him the title of the world's best discus thrower.
76 Olympics.com.

PART 2:

West
to
Northwestern

KENNETH L. WILSON
Director
1923

Wilson in 1923 while serving as athletic director
at Drake University

CHAPTER 8

Farming or Athletics?

Tug made mental notes of every aspect of the Olympic competitions he watched, not really cognizant of just why he was doing so. He analyzed strategies and techniques used by different athletes and how each competition had been organized. Some athletes who appeared rather nonchalant about competing had surprised him. It wasn't until he saw a particular athlete saunter to the ring and win on his first throw that Tug realized it was pure confidence, not indifference, that he witnessed. Competing in the games had been a dream come true and he wanted to remember every detail. An invitation to stay in Europe a few more weeks to compete in Paris and London as part of a touring American team extended that dream. He was beginning to live the experiences he previously had only heard about from others. He enjoyed every moment because he realized the chance of making athletics a career was slim. Those thoughts kept him occupied as he traveled back to America on the Red Star Line passenger ship in early September. This time his accommodations were first class and included a dinner menu with liver paste, salmon, roasted capon, potatoes, spinach, squash, salad, pudding, and ice cream.[77]

---

77 Original paper menu preserved and is now a part of the Tug Wilson memorabilia collection at the Atwood-Hammond Public Library.

Tug felt certain he was destined to return to the family farm. With his college diploma in hand, Tug settled upon the idea of accepting a job as a county farm advisor. It was a safe, logical decision, he thought; besides, he didn't have any other offers. That changed unexpectedly when he dropped by Illinois athletics director George Huff's office to recount his Olympic adventure. Huff listened intently, obviously impressed, and then tilted back his chair when the conversation finally ended.

"Do you have a job yet?" he asked.

"Nothing in sight," Tug replied.

He wasn't quite sure why he didn't tell Huff about the advisor position.

"How would you like to come in here and help us in the athletic department?" Huff asked. "I think we could put you to very good use."[78]

The offer stunned Tug into silence. He considered Huff a friend and admired his coaching and administrative acumen. In return, Huff likely saw a little bit of himself in Tug. Huff, a farm boy born in Champaign, loved baseball and played football for the first time for the Fighting Illini in 1888. His coaching career at Illinois began before Tug was born. Now, as twenty-four-year-old Tug sat in his office, Huff was in the middle of a four-decade tenure that molded Illinois into a nationally prominent sports program. His leadership and keen eye for hiring coaches with character and talent—Gill, Jones, and Zuppke, to name a few—helped create championship teams and earned him the title of "father of Illini athletics."[79]

Huff recognized some promising characteristics in Tug and believed he could be a great asset to Illinois by promoting athletics throughout the Midwest. He believed athletic competition offered enormous benefits but didn't receive enough attention from community newspapers. He wanted

---

78 *The Big Ten*, 145.
79 Fightingillini.com Hall of Fame biography.

Tug to help spread the word by submitting weekly articles about Illinois teams.

"I think you are just the person who can do that," he told Tug.[80]

The job included assisting Coach Jones with the freshman football team. Tug didn't give a second thought about the farm advisor post. It thrilled him to accept Huff's offer. His position at Illinois provided opportunities to work on his decision-making skills and to meet people he could learn from and help his career. Huff introduced Tug to John L. Griffith, who had been hired to lead the Illinois coaching school. Griffith, a former Army major, had been in charge of physical fitness training for the entire US Army during World War I and strongly believed athletics, especially football, had an important role in preparing future soldiers. Griffith hoped to instill the importance of youth physical fitness to other college and high school coaches through the coaching school. Tug's job was to introduce Griffith—often referred to as "Major Griffith"—to student groups on campus, so he could promote the importance of coaching and physical fitness and possibly recruit students into those fields.

It wasn't long before Griffith tried his recruiting skills on Tug, encouraging him to apply for the position of athletics director at Drake University in Des Moines, Iowa. During Griffith's nine-year tenure there, he coached football and founded the Drake Relays, a spring track event that became respected nationwide for its slate of first-rate competitors.

"I'm sure you can handle the position," Griffith told him.[81]

Tug was stunned. He considered himself too young and too inexperienced. Griffith was making a mistake, he thought.

"Here I was, just twenty-four years old, and someone whose judgment I respected was suggesting I was ready to head up

---

80 *The Big Ten*, 145.
81 *The Big Ten*, 146.

the entire sports program at one of the finest colleges in the Midwest," Tug later recalled.[82]

Griffith insisted and set up an interview despite Tug's hesitance. The interview with the Drake athletic board was what Tug expected. The board members politely asked some personal questions while expressing doubt about his inexperience. It seemed the trip to Iowa had been a waste of time, but the members asked Tug to stay long enough to discuss ideas for improving Drake's athletic program at an alumni dinner. Tug obliged. Feeling the pressure lift from his shoulders, he relaxed and informally addressed the guests. His thoughts about what Drake University athletics could or should be kept his audience's attention and gave the board members a reason to rethink the situation. When he finished, the audience applauded enthusiastically, and the impressed board members quickly huddled with some influential alumni. They called Tug into another meeting before he left town the next day; he was the school's newest athletics director.

Everything seemed to have happened so fast. In the span of one year, Tug had come within a whisker of starting a career in farming only to be swept into a job at his alma mater and then into an administration position at a major university. Tug could barely contain his excitement about the course his life had taken. His love for learning, playing sports, coaching, and working to build winning teams all rolled into a career. "I knew, now, that athletic administration was the thing that would always hold my most intense interest," he recalled.[83]

---

82 *The Big Ten*, 146
83 *The Big Ten*, 147.

"I knew, now, that athletic administration was the thing that would always hold my most intense interest."

Tug Wilson

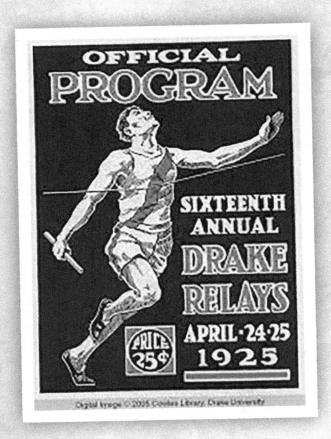

OFFICIAL PROGRAM

SIXTEENTH ANNUAL DRAKE RELAYS

PRICE 25¢

APRIL·24·25 1925

Digital Image © 2005 Cowles Library, Drake University

1925 Drake Relays program cover
(Drake University Archives & Special Collections)

CHAPTER 9

Elevating Drake Athletics

Drake University, a private institute founded in 1881 by a teacher and a former Union Civil War general,[84] sits in the heart of Des Moines, the capital city of Iowa. It is the home of the second oldest law school west of the Mississippi River and home of the renowned Drake Relays. Griffith's legacy at Drake included the school's team name. They had been known as the Ducklings, the Ganders, and even the Drakes before a newspaper reporter noticed Coach Griffith brought his pet bulldogs to every practice. Bulldogs, he called the team, and the name stuck.[85] Even today, the school's live mascot—a bulldog named Griff—honors the former coach.

Although over 350 miles apart, Tug found Des Moines much like Champaign-Urbana—a growing cultural oasis in a sea of grain fields. Drake's reputation in the fields of law, journalism, and business anchored the institution, but school officials also wanted to gain notoriety in athletics. When Tug arrived in 1922, Drake's athletic teams were one of the "weak

---

84 Teacher-preacher George T. Carpenter and Francis Marion Drake, a general, railroad magnate, and former Iowa governor, started the school initially affiliated with the Christian Church (Disciples of Christ).
85 En.Wikipedia.org. Drake Bulldog History.

sisters"[86] in the Missouri Valley Conference and had yet to break into the ranks as a national contender. Tug quickly recognized what he faced as Drake's athletic director: helping a small school realize its ambitious athletic aims. Elevating Drake's athletic program offered quite a challenge for anyone in their first job as a leader whose decisions could bear great consequences, both good and bad. Whatever apprehension Tug may have experienced about his new role, though, likely was overshadowed by the confidence others had in his abilities. Tug knew he had learned from some of the best people in the profession and could rely upon their advice if needed. He was up for the challenge and approached it with gusto.

Tug's first plan of action involved developing a new attitude among the players and coaches. He promoted optimism, determination, and quality performance through personal interaction with every team member, including helping coach some teams. Tug also involved himself in the community, bolstering his teams via interaction with supporters and fans. Soon, the program began attracting more quality players and coaches to train them. Drake's football team, coached by Ossie Solem, ended the 1921 season 5–2—the best school record in nearly ten years. The next season, the Bulldogs went undefeated. Drake's golf team was first to gain national prominence for the school when it captured Big Ten championship[87] titles in 1920 and 1921.

Tug also focused on building upon Griffith's creation, the Drake Relays. In its inaugural year in 1910, the event fielded eighty-two high school and collegiate competitors despite blizzard conditions. The event took on a circus-like atmosphere with high school and college teams pitching tents in the infield. Despite a limited budget and materials, Tug wanted to attract a competitive field for the relays and had

---

86 *The Decatur Daily Review*, December 29, 1922, 8.
87 Although Drake was not a member of the Big Ten, it was allowed to compete in that conference.

high hopes of producing a championship team from Drake as well. In 1922, he expanded the relays to a two-day event, attracting over 10,000 fans to the cinder track at the Drake Bowl. It became the first major track and field event to be broadcast live on the radio.[88]

The Drake Relays always had been conducted in April, the week before the Penn Relays at the University of Pennsylvania. Until the early 1920s, the Penn Relays, the oldest and largest competition of its kind in the nation, was considered the premier track and field event. Tug wanted to compete for the attention, moving the Drake Relays to the same day as the Penn Relays. He bounced the idea off of three Big Ten Conference administrators before making the final decision. He also invited the "cream of the crop" amateur athletes to compete, a move that attracted more fans. For track and field athletes, the Drake Relays were a premier event that offered a springboard to the Olympics.[89]

In 1924, Tug invited his former Olympic teammate, Charley Paddock, known then as the world's fastest human, to compete. In an article published in the Des Moines *Evening Tribune*, Paddock proclaimed Des Moines as a leading athletic city of the world. "But in the year 1924, neither London nor New York will be able to hold a meet which can rank with the Drake Relays," he proclaimed. Paddock set a world record—12.0 seconds in a special 125-yard race—during the relays. Tug also got local leaders on board to build a new 18,000-seat stadium that premiered in 1925. During Tug's tenure at Drake, the relays grew to include over twenty-six events, two thousand competitors, and thousands of fans.[90]

---

88 En.Wikipedia.org. Drake Relay history.
89 Logue, Andrew. 2016. "Drake Relays Boast Impressive History as Olympic Springboard." Desmoinesregister.com, April 27, 2016.
90 Famous relay participants include Jesse Owens, Carl Lewis, Usain Bolt, Bruce Jenner, and Wilma Rudolph. It is not uncommon for national and world records to be broken at this event.

Amateur Athlete Controversy

Managing the Drake Relays helped Tug expand his network of individuals and organizations who shared his support for amateur athletics. Working with the Amateur Athletic Union (AAU) was an important part of his job, especially concerning the Drake Relays. The organization created in 1888 worked to establish common standards and uniformity in amateur sports and certified athletes with the amateur status. In other words, amateur athletes could not be paid a salary or receive substantial prizes or rewards for their performance. Tug believed in this principle for amateur athletes, but his resolve would be tested time after time during his career.

Tug fired a shot of contention against paying amateurs while attempting to reach an agreement with Hugo Quist, the manager for two Finnish runners, Paavo Nurmi and Ville Ritola, known as the "Flying Finns." During the 1924 Olympics in Paris, France, Nurmi earned five gold medals and Ritola won four gold and two silver medals in medium-and long-distance races. Both were headline competitors during an American tour in 1925, and Tug was eager for a commitment to the Drake Relays. Under the AAU,[91] sponsors could only pay certain travel expenses, but Tug claimed Quist demanded $1,500 for the Finns to compete. Tug told reporters the demand was exorbitant and violated the spirit of amateur sports. "When it comes to the point of hiring stars to make a meet successful it is not keeping faith with amateur rules," Tug said.[92] He filed an affidavit with the AAU detailing encounters with Quist, specifically a meeting under the bleachers at the Loyola University Relays in Chicago. Tug said he and Quist

---

91 Athletes competing in amateur competitions were allowed $7 a day for hotel and other living costs, as well as travel expenses to and from the event. Officials later increased that amount to $10 a day.

92 *Des Moines Register*. 1925. "Finn Distance Star Will Not Run at Relays." April 22, 1925, 1.

negotiated using a slip of paper[93] passed back and forth. Tug said Quist raised his fingers at four consecutive offers. Tug's final offer was $250. "Double it and it will be all right," Tug quoted Quist as saying. It was then that Tug said he quit. "I told him the deal was off then as we wanted to keep the Drake Relays an amateur event."[94] Quist told reporters he had only met Tug once, "and the expenses of Nurmi and Ritola positively were not discussed between us."[95]

When the controversy made newspaper headlines around the country, national AAU secretary Frederick Rubien claimed Tug's story was a "publicity stunt."[96] In May 1925, an AAU investigative committee issued a statement clearing Quist and the two Finn runners, but also reprimanding Tug. "Wilson . . . should be censured for engaging a representative to obtain Nurmi's entry and for making an offer to Nurmi . . . [which] is a violation of all amateur rules."[97] Tug wasn't surprised by the finding, claiming the investigation was a "whitewash" (better known as a cover-up) and that Rubien had "assumed the role of defender rather than investigator."[98]

In retrospect, Tug likely didn't realize that admitting to offering $250 put him rather than Quist in the investigator's spotlight. His heart was in the right place even though his actions suggested otherwise.

---

93 *Des Moines Tribune*. 1925. "Quist Denies Drake's Claim." April 25, 1925, 1. Tug offered to give AAU investigators the slip of paper as proof. Officials at the University of Chicago claimed Quist requested $1,000 but other universities denied he made such a demand.
94 *Des Moines Tribune*, April 25, 1925, 1.
95 Pittsburgh *Post Gazette*. 1925. "Quist Reiterates Denial." April 25, 1925, 13.
96 Reno *Gazette-Journal*. 1925. "Expenses Demand Will Be Sifted." April 25, 1925, 2.
97 Associated Press *Sunday News* (Lancaster, Pennsylvania). 1925. "Nurmi Cleared of All Professional Charges." May 10, 1925, 11.
98 Associated Press, *Chicago Tribune*. 1925. "Tug Wilson Says A.A.U. Defended Nurmi In Quiz." May 11, 1925, 26.

From Drake to Northwestern

Interest in the controversy soon faded. That summer, Tug was preparing for another sports season in Iowa when he received a call from his old friend Griffith, who had left the University of Illinois shortly after Tug had. Athletics directors within the Big Ten Conference needed help to control growing problems with eligibility issues and recruiting practices. They hired Griffith as its first commissioner to promote educational campaigns on amateurism and investigate intercollegiate athletic problems. Griffith told Tug he had recommended him to Northwestern University to succeed athletics director Dana "Doc" Evans, who died unexpectedly of a heart attack in November 1924. A committee, chaired by O. F. Long, had been taking its time in a nationwide search for a successor. When they investigated Griffith's recommendation, they found Tug's counterparts throughout the country held him in high regard. "We have been advised that his brother directors think well of him for thorough methods, for his efficiency, his high principles and gentlemanly [manner]," Long said in a typed statement.[99] Even Drake President Daniel W. Morehouse praised Tug for putting "new life into our intramural athletics" and gaining support from both faculty and students. "Since he came here the attendance and receipts at our relays have trebled and the number of participants has doubled," Morehouse said.[100]

After meeting with Northwestern president Walter Dill Scott and the search committee in Chicago, Tug was offered the job. In a statement released later, Long said Tug's previous athletic accomplishments and his administrative experience were exactly what the committee had been looking for. "Mr. Wilson has the advantage of youthful enthusiasm and

99 Original press release from Northwestern University dated June 27, 1925. Part of Tug Wilson collection at Atwood-Hammond Public Library.
100 Original press release from Northwestern University dated June 27, 1925. Part of Tug Wilson collection at Atwood-Hammond Public Library.

vision, coupled with successful experience in George Huff's organization at Illinois as well as in his own work at Drake," Long said.

Uncertain about what to do, Tug consulted Drake University officials about his current contract, and then he went to see Huff. Everyone he consulted urged to him to accept a position they believed was a big step up the career ladder. Still, he wasn't sure. He was thrilled with his progress at Drake, and yet he respected Griffith's support. After all, he gave Tug a leg up into the field of athletic administration. His final decision, however, depended on the opinion of one other person, his wife, Dorothy.

Despite enjoying the challenges the Drake position posed, Tug could barely tolerate being away from Dorothy Shade, his college sweetheart. After graduating from Illinois, Dorothy accepted a teaching position in the Bloomington-Normal area of Illinois, just fifteen miles southwest of her hometown of Lexington. Tug spent many long weekends and most of his summers continuing their courtship, but it wasn't enough. On January 1, 1923, they were married in a small but quaint ceremony, accompanied by a harpist, at the home of Dorothy's parents in Normal. The newspaper announcement of the marriage described Dorothy as a "prominent, young socialite."[101]

Tug told Dorothy about the job offer at Northwestern, expressing some doubt about taking on such a challenging job when he felt secure with his position at Drake. But the thought of returning to their home state was enticing. Dorothy didn't hesitate when he finally asked her opinion. "When do we leave?" she asked.

---

101 *The Daily Pentagraph* (Bloomington, Illinios). 1923. "Shade-Wilson Wedding Today." January 1, 1923, 8.

Tug Wilson was named athletic director of
Northwestern University on September 18, 1925.

CHAPTER 10

Tenure at Northwestern

Chicagoland—the common name for Chicago and its metropolitan area—includes the city of Evanston, the home of Northwestern University. A group of Methodist business leaders including John Evans, Orrington Lunt, and Grant Goodrich founded the university on the North Shore of Lake Michigan in 1851 before Evanston was even incorporated. The city, named after Evans, made its mark as a wealthy Chicago suburb because of a steel manufacturing company[102] that supplied equipment for water wells and for oil fields around the world. Even today, Evanston is considered one of top five wealthiest cities in the Midwest.

Northwestern prided itself on being a leader in intellectual learning, especially in private research and education. School officials also wanted to be nationally recognized in athletics and were in the position to do so under Tug, whose career in athletics coincided with a remarkable time in collegiate sports history. As an athletics director, all collegiate sports at Northwestern fell under his purview, and he did his best to

---

102 "Clayton Mark & Company History." en.Wikipedia.com. The company manufactured steel pipe and tubes for water wells and the oil industry all over the world. It contributed about $10 million annually to the city's economy. The company was sold to Youngstown Sheet and Tube in 1923.

improve them all. But it was football that garnered most of his attention since the game continued to grow tremendously in America, both in its development and in its popularity, during the first part of the twentieth century.

The Early Days of American Football

American football, also known as gridiron football, can trace its roots to an odd marriage between rugby and soccer that premiered as a college sport in 1869 on the East Coast. Today's fans likely wouldn't have recognized that game between Rutgers College and the College of New Jersey (now known as Princeton) as football at all. Teams of an unlimited number of players attempted to advance the ball by kicking or swatting it. Lacking regulation, the game was reminiscent of the medieval game of mob football, a violent match in which injuries were common. It wasn't until 1873 that students at Yale, Columbia, Princeton, and Rutgers joined forces in creating the Intercollegiate Football Association[103] in an effort to standardize the game. It was a Yale medical student, Walter Camp, who revolutionized it by emphasizing speed over strength. His introduction of the line of scrimmage, down and distance rules, blocking, the forward pass, and other contributions earned him the title of the "Father of American Football."[104]

In 1879, the University of Michigan became the first college west of Pennsylvania to establish a football team. Northwestern, University of Minnesota, Purdue University, University of Wisconsin, University of Illinois, and University of Chicago followed within the next three years. In 1895, those schools created the first college league, the Intercollegiate Conference of Faculty Representatives, later known as the Western Conference and eventually the Big Ten.

---

103 Walter Camp playing career, en.wikipedia.com.
104 "'The Father of American Football' is Born—Today in History: April 7," connecticuthistory.org.

The conference, anchored by Michigan, the first western football powerhouse, established national dominance during the 1930s and 1940s. During those two decades, Minnesota claimed five national titles; Michigan, three; and Ohio State, one.[105]

Future Hall of Fame coaches Amos Alonzo Stagg of the University of Chicago, Stanford's Glenn "Pop" Warner, Knute Rockne at Notre Dame, and others also made significant contributions. Stagg introduced the huddle, the tackling dummy, and the pre-snap shift.[106] Warner created the three-point stance, the single/double wing formation, and the body block.[107] And Rockne popularized the forward pass.[108]

From the administrative perspective, the growing popularity of football represented a potential cash cow for their respective schools. Larger audiences increased gate receipts, but attracting those audiences depended upon a variety of factors. Winning was the key, but it required the right combination of talented coaches and athletes, hired and recruited with the help of an athletics director. Winning created positive publicity, opened the pocketbooks of alumni, and attracted more students, athletic and otherwise. Despite its humble beginnings, football has become the major source of revenue for athletic programs in public and private schools in America today.[109]

Making Northwestern Athletics Respectable

When twenty-nine-year-old Tug came to Northwestern in 1925, the school was the smallest and one of only two private institutes in a conference that now employed the youngest athletics director. In that position, Tug was tasked with

---

105 Ohio State joined the Big Ten in 1912.
106 "Amos Alonzo Stagg." athletics.uchicago.edu.
107 "Glenn 'Pop' Warner." georgiaencyclopedia.org.
108 "Knute Rockne." Britannica.com.
109 "Organization of Football in the United States." newworldencyclopedia.org.

coordinating multiple facets like arms on an octopus. He and his staff not only dealt with players and coaches, but alumni, school and conference administrators, regulators, and fans. He oversaw Northwestern's physical education department as well, a role he considered vitally important to the health and welfare of all students. The responsibility for molding Northwestern into an athletic powerhouse in its own right was a responsibility Tug was willing and able to assume.

Northwestern's athletic teams were known simply as "Purple," although behind their back competitors called them "The Fighting Methodists." A Chicago sports reporter later referred to its football team as a "purple wall of wildcats"[110] and the name stuck. The Wildcats also had the poorest record in the conference with no championship titles in football, baseball, or track since 1903. Tug also realized he had inherited numerous problems: eligibility issues, an over-involved alumni group, flagrant Big Ten rule violations, and poor facilities. Their dismal athletic record and the fact that Northwestern had higher tuition fees and generally higher entrance requirements than its sister schools certainly didn't help recruiting efforts. The situation somewhat surprised Tug, who had expected better. "I was the most disillusioned man in American sports,"[111] Tug recalled. He knew setting things right in the athletics department would not be easy, but he was confident he could help guide it back onto a straighter path and produce respected, quality athletic teams just had he done at Drake.

On his first day on campus, Tug headed straight to the old Patten Gym to meet with coaches and to take stock of the overall climate within the department. It seemed roles had reversed for Tug. He was dressed smartly in a suit, vest, and tie while standing before a group of men, each of whom was more

---

110 "The Early History of the Wildcat Nickname." hailtopurple.com.
111 *The Big Ten,* 159.

than a decade older than him. Ironically, Tug was only about ten years older than most of the collegiate athletes. The players and coaches, however, couldn't help but respect the young man whose reputation as an Olympic athlete and a successful administrator preceded him.

Tug didn't want to start off on the wrong foot in a new conference, so he paid Commissioner Griffith a visit to confess the rule violations he had uncovered and questionable financial issues. "I didn't want to start my career at Northwestern with that hanging over me," he recalled.[112] Griffith understood Tug's need to start with a clean slate, suggesting Tug meet with Northwestern's president and financial managers to develop of plan of action, which they did. Tug then took a road trip, hoping to pick the brains of those whom he considered the leading athletic directors in the conference: Huff at Illinois, L. W. St. John at Ohio State, Fielding Yost at Michigan, and Stagg in Chicago.[113] The tour not only bolstered Tug's enthusiasm, but he returned with a pile of suggestions and ideas to improve his program.

Before he could begin developing long-term plans for the school, Tug focused on putting out some other fires. With the help of some younger faculty members, Tug spent the summer whipping the football team into shape academically. Nearly two dozen members of the team were failing their classes, jeopardizing the school's ability to field a team for the 1925 season. He was determined to make them eligible legitimately or not at all. Relentless tutoring saved the season, with all but two boys regaining their eligibility. "I was proud of the big group that did," Tug said.[114] The team recorded its best

---

112 *The Big Ten,* 160.
113 All legendary coaches and players. St. John was named to the Naismith Memorial Basketball Hall of Fame. Yost and Stagg were inducted into the Collage Football Hall of Fame.
114 *The Big Ten,* 161.

record $(5-3)$[115] in eight years and included a 3–2 upset over the Michigan Wolverines at Soldier Field in Chicago.

On November 7, 1925, those two teams took to the boggy field during a relentless torrential rainstorm. As Tug recalled, opposing coach Yost suggested he postpone the game, but the much-anticipated match had sold over 75,000 tickets. "I thought we should play," he said. "I told Yost the 50,000 fans (who showed up) had a right to see a game."[116] Field conditions were so bad, officials couldn't draw all the chalk lines, and referees frequently called time-out to wipe mud off the ball. Sheets of rain, puddles of water, and nearly six inches of slimy, shoe-sucking mud shut down the Wolverines' formidable passing game. In fact, the Wolverines recorded only one pass, and it was incomplete. Fumbles were so frequent neither team could even convert a first down. It was "one of the best swimming matches Michigan has ever entered," according to a *Chicago Daily Tribune* article. The Wildcats prevailed with a wind-assisted field goal that barely cleared the uprights and an intentional safety—an unexpected, but clever move that put the ball back in the hands of the Wolverines with hopes of another fumble. The 3–2 win handed the nationally ranked Wolverines their only loss for the season and made Northwestern the only team to put numbers on the board against a team that outscored its opponents 227–3 that year. "It was an incredible game," Tug said. "I would see hundreds more in my lifetime but this one I'd never forget."[117]

The Wildcats' successful season prompted a massive gathering a few weeks later.[118] As many as three thousand Northwestern students celebrated the season by starting

---

115 Under Coach Glenn Thistlethwaite from 1922–1926.

116 *The Big Ten*, 163.

117 *The Big Ten*, 163.

118 Some news reports indicate the Northwestern students felt their team had earned a share of the conference championship, while other students were enraged about reports that Coach Yost had given his players gold emblems to commemorate winning the conference.

bonfires, dancing, and cheering in the streets and around the Evanston downtown plaza. Conflicting news accounts characterized the gathering as a rally of disgruntled fans angry that conference officials didn't name the Wildcats cochampions. When Evanston police and fire officials attempted to intervene, the event turned into a riot, with law enforcement officers firing tear bombs. Riot squads from Chicago police departments and war veterans were called to assist the local police force. Tug joined Wildcats' standouts Tim Lowry and Ralph "Moon" Baker in an attempt to quell the disturbance. Reminiscent of his days as the student president at Illinois,[119] Tug jumped on top of a car and in a calming voice urged the crowd to douse the fires and refrain from violence or destruction. He even suggested they fall in line for a snake dance. The crowd cheered but declined to comply.

The three-hour rally in the aristocratic town turned into a riot, ending with a burned vacant fraternity house, the Evanston mayor being hit in the head, injured police officers, overturned cars, and a handful of arrests. The next day, a telegram arrived at the office of the University of Michigan's president. The message was signed by Walter Dill Scott, president at Northwestern; Coach Glenn Thistlethwaite; administrative officials; the board of trustees; and Lowry, the team captain; it unequivocally proclaimed Michigan the sole owner of the conference title despite a call for joint honors. "Northwestern makes no claim for any share . . . but regards it as a privilege, even for a few minutes, to be placed in the class with the University of Michigan."[120]

---

119 During one instance, Tug was called upon to prevent a potential violent situation involving members of the sophomore class attempting to haze a group of freshmen who had taken over the Orpheum Theatre. Tug convinced the two groups to clash somewhere else.
120 *Chicago Tribune.* 1925. "N.U. Concedes Big Ten Title to Wolverines." November 25, 1925, 21.

Evanston officials, however, weren't very forgiving. They contended Northwestern should pay for the $500 worth of tear gas police used against the rioters and indicated the school's plan for a new stadium was in jeopardy.

Priming the Pipeline

Tug also toured the high schools in and around Chicago and realized that Northwestern, unlike other neighboring institutions, had very few graduates in the coaching field. He wanted the pipeline of resources that coaches could bring to Northwestern. Linking with more high schools could improve recruiting efforts for top players as well as coaches. Recalling his days in Illinois, Tug created a low-cost, two-week summer coaching school at Northwestern. The camps provided training in football, basketball, track, and administration for coaches who couldn't afford the longer, more expensive camps elsewhere. Northwestern's dormitories provided housing and the Chicago Cubs and White Sox organizations provided complimentary tickets for nearby games as added incentives. Tug also enlisted the help of notable coaches, including Zuppke, Warner, and Rockne. Coaches from high schools, colleges, and universities came from all over the United States, growing the event from 160 coaches the first year to 480 the next. "The response was almost unbelievable," Tug recalled. "Over the years many fine athletes came to Northwestern as a result of contacts we'd made with high school coaches at our annual coaching school."[121]

Tug also could place some of the more successful coaches in college jobs. "As I look back over a long athletic career, these memories bring some of my happiest moments," he wrote years later.

---

121 *The Big Ten*, 169–170.

"Age of Stadium Building"

The end of World War I ushered in a new decade, the Roaring Twenties, known for its economic prosperity and a new cultural identity for Americans, especially in cities like Chicago. In collegiate athletics, the 1920s became known as the "Age of Stadium Building."[122] Returning soldiers flocked to enroll in colleges, bringing their thirst for competition with them. Intercollegiate athletics, especially football, became extremely popular since there was little professional football played in the United States at the time. Radio and television were still in their infancy. "Consequently, the only way to enjoy a football game was to go and see it," Tug recalled.[123]

Attendance at collegiate football games exploded with alumni and visitors filling outdated stadiums to over capacity. The competition on the field wasn't the only action either. Big Ten marching bands developed intricate field formations to entertain the crowds—the beginning of a tradition that spread throughout the country. Homecoming[124] became popular too as administrators recognized it as a way to draw alumni back to campus and contribute to development funds. The pressure for vastly larger stadiums fueled the construction movement.

More seats equaled more gate receipts—a much-needed influx of cash for schools. In response to the growing needs, seven new Big Ten facilities were built during the 1920s. "These magnificent stadia were to play a very important part in the athletic history of the Big Ten," Tug later wrote. "The increased capacity brought in tremendous revenue, and this revenue was plowed right back into the athletic departments and into sports that had little crowd appeal."[125]

At Drake, Tug oversaw construction of an 18,000-seat stadium which opened in 1925. Northwestern officials realized

---

122 *The Big Ten*, 192.
123 *The Big Ten*, 192.
124 The tradition was created by the University of Illinois before World War I.
125 *The Big Ten*, 193.

that year it had outgrown its 10,000-seat wooden bleachers—the same ones that narrowly escaped being burned during the riot. After the riot, Evanston officials threated to reject a building permit request for the project but later relented. Northwestern announced plans to build a new $1.4 million stadium before the next season. The project, under the direction of Northwestern's business manager, William A. Dyche, consisted of building the first fully concrete, multitiered stadium in the conference with over four times the seating capacity. Construction added to an already hectic year for Tug, who spent hours finalizing last-minute details with architects.

At Northwestern, over 45,000 fans attended the dedication ceremony and christened Dyche Stadium on November 13, 1926, during a game against the University of Chicago. The outcome was more successful than the pregame dedication ceremony. As Tug recalled, invited dignitaries made their speeches to a dead loudspeaker system despite the school using the best available microphones and testing the entire system repeatedly hours before the game. Purple fans, however, were treated to a remarkable 88-yard touchdown run by Vic Gustafson in the opening kickoff. He scored three more touchdowns in the 38–7 win—a victory ten years in the making. Northwestern went undefeated in the conference that year and tied with Michigan for its first Western Conference championship title. The Wildcats shared the title again in 1930 and 1931, but claimed it as their own in 1936.

Promoting Football

Tug exhibited a knack for promoting football, especially the Wildcats, drawing crowds and solving problems. In 1933, when the World's Fair was in Chicago, fair directors announced they wanted an athletic event to attract crowds. Previous attempts to premier track events had failed to draw the desired attention. Tug and Wildcats' Coach Dick Hanley planned on pitting two teams of the best college seniors from schools in the east and west against each other in the first ever all-star game. The event was financed through Northwestern's summer coaching school with support from the railroads for transportation, sports writers who provided free publicity, and fair announcers who persuaded fairgoers to attend in the final hours before kickoff. Hanley coached the East team and Howard Jones of Southern California coached the West. Organizers expected about 45,000 fans, but when thousands crashed through the gates at the last moment, Tug estimated over 52,000 fans watched the East defeat the West 13–7. Despite early concerns the event wouldn't turn a profit, it netted nearly $13,000, benefitting Northwestern's student loan fund and the coaching school.[126]

Tug started another conference "first" in October 1935 when Northwestern was scheduled to host Purdue. Unfortunately, the afternoon kickoff conflicted with the Chicago Cubs' World Series game against the Detroit Tigers in Chicago. Tug feared Northwestern would lose attendance, so he moved the football game to a night start. No lights? No problem. Tug ordered flood lights, had them attached to telephone poles, and placed them around the playing field. Although Purdue won 7–0 before 30,000 fans, Northwestern went down in the record books as having the first night game in conference history.

Promoting Physical Fitness

Tug's responsibilities as athletics director also involved physical activities and training through the school's physical education department and the US Navy's V-12 program. Like Griffith, Tug believed sports could play an integral role in preparing young men for military service. In announcing

---

126 Arch Ward, sports editor for the *Chicago Tribune*, continued the all-star game after Big Ten faculty representatives and athletic directors voted to forbid any director or football coach to sponsor such promotions. In 1934, the all-star game matched collegiate athletes against the Chicago Bears.

Northwestern's compulsory physical education program, Tug urged every student to engage in "the spirit of the program."[127]

"We hope to bring home to every student at Northwestern the belief that physical development and enjoyable recreation can be obtained at one and the same time," Tug said. "He who properly balances study and play will be the best student."[128] The program required all 2,800 undergraduates to dedicate at least four and a half hours each week to body conditioning, competitive sports, gymnastic stunts, swimming, or obstacle course races.

One morning a Chicago newspaper photographer captured Tug and a group of Northwestern students running through the icy water along the Lake Michigan shore as part of the program. "Play the game you like and learn to play that you may become stronger, healthier men who will be a credit to Northwestern University and your nation," said Tug, who later boasted the program engaged eighty percent of the male students in intramural sports.[129]

Tug's dedication to youth fitness would later earn him a position with the President's Council on Youth Fitness. President Dwight Eisenhower established the school-based, comprehensive program in 1956 to promote health and regular physical activity. Tug's service on the council continued during John F. Kennedy's presidency.[130]

Tug also sustained a twelve-year relationship with the Chicago Board of Education, working as a paid advisor for its physical fitness program. He helped reorganize the district's physical education department, monitored compliance with rules and regulations, purchased equipment, and reduced expenses. His role, however, was criticized by *Chicago Daily News* editors who said Tug had an "easy money job"[131] because, as they claimed, he did

---

127 Northwestern University promotional material, undated, (Tug Wilson memorabilia collection at Atwood-Hammond Public Library).
128 Northwestern University promotional material.
129 Northwestern University promotional material.
130 Tug received an invitation to Eisenhower's second inauguration in 1957.
131 *Chicago Daily News*. [1952]. "Big Ten Czar Worked 11 Years for City Board of Education." July 28, [year].

President Eisenhower with Tug. Eisenhower had
invited Tug to the presidential inauguration.

little or nothing to earn his $4,000 annual salary. Northwestern
administrators who had approved his second job, Chicago
school administrators, and even a rival newspaper contended
that Tug had earned every penny. Tug took the criticism all
in stride, having become accustomed to newspaper reports
about various aspects of his life, especially in Chicago, which
supported at least three major daily newspapers. Reporters
and photographers chronicled his attendance at major events
and conferences, his speaking engagements, and even when he
suffered the flu. In 1933, an Associated Press report[132] detailed
Tug's encounter with a runaway car that rolled down a hill and
struck his vehicle. Tug leaped from his car just moments before
impact. Neither Tug nor the barking dog occupying the other

---

132 Associated Press/*The Post-Crescent* (Appleton, Wisconsin). "'Tug'" Wilson Car
Is Damaged in Accident." October 17, 1933, 11.

vehicle were injured. More than a decade later, Tug and his wife escaped unharmed from a burning fraternity house they stayed at while visiting Tulane University in New Orleans. The couple fled the house wearing only their nightclothes. That event also made headlines in the *Chicago Tribune*.[133]

Can We Fight and Play?

America's entry into World War II in 1941 prompted military officials to call upon universities across the nation to accommodate soldiers with housing and training facilities. In 1943, the US War Department instituted the Navy V-12 program on campuses nationwide, hoping to maintain a continuous supply of officers. Northwestern, which is about twenty miles south of Naval Station Great Lakes, the nation's largest training station, provided physical training for one thousand men assigned to their unit. Military service also drained the pool of potential athletes and led some universities to drop their football programs, some permanently. As many as fifty-two colleges opted out in the 1942 season alone, according to the Associated Press.[134] To help fill the void, Big Ten officials temporarily lifted the ban on freshmen playing varsity and revised other eligibility rules, but critics still questioned the advisability of playing sports at all during the time of war. Tug supported the war effort in any way he could, but he insisted conference officials should not cancel the season. Sports offered physical and mental assets for players and their country, he said. "The lessons these boys learned in football and other sports now helps them become better soldiers," Tug said. "They need courage, spirit, and rugged constitution in this big fight—the same requirement in sports."

---

133 *Chicago Tribune.* 1942. "Mr. and Mrs. Tug Wilson Escape Injury in Fire." January 3, 1942, 18.

134 "52 Colleges Dropping Football for War," by Associated Press writer Harold Claassen, in an undated newspaper article referenced in "Like 2020, college football was very different during World War II," Brenden Welper, www.cache. ncaa.com, accessed October 7, 2020.

Watching sports also served as an "escape valve" for fans. "Hundreds of thousands each week watch football and forget for an hour or two these troublous times."[135]

Northwestern only won one game in 1942 but bounced back to post a 6–2 record the next season with the help of future NFL Hall of Fame quarterback, Otto Graham, and running back, Bill DeCorrevont. Graham was attending Northwestern on a basketball scholarship when football coach "Pappy" Waldorf saw him throwing during an intramural football game. Waldorf recruited Graham, who set a passing record of eighty-nine completions in a single season and a career high of 2,132 passing yards in the Big Ten.[136] Both players enlisted for military service. Graham continued to play for the Wildcats while waiting to be called for duty in the US Coast Guard. DeCorrevont joined the Navy and played football for various "service teams" created at bases nationwide, including the Bluejackets at Naval Station Great Lakes near Chicago. Northwestern, with Graham at the helm, defeated the Bluejackets 13–0 in 1943.

Improving Northwestern's Basketball Program

Football, of course, wasn't the only intercollegiate sport played at Northwestern. Tug felt confident with the coaches over swimming and track. Swim coach Tom Robinson, who Tug considered the dean of the athletic staff, produced the best record in the conference with ten Big Ten titles, five National Collegiate Athletic Association (NCAA) championships, and eleven Olympic performers during his tenure at Northwestern.[137] Tug focused his attention on building up Northwestern's coaching staff in other sports. His search for a new basketball coach took longer than expected, but he

---

135 Siler, Tom, 1943. "'Tug' Wilson Lauds Football in Wartime." *Chicago Tribune*, July 7, 1943.
136 "Otto Graham." en.wikipedia.org.
137 "Coach Tom Robinson." swimmingcoach.org.

found what he was looking for in A. C. "Dutch" Lonborg. It didn't take long for Lonborg to produce a Wildcats team that claimed the school's first undisputed championship in 1931. When Tug took the helm, Northwestern had the nation's best field house and played host to the annual indoor track and field conference meet. In 1939, Northwestern hosted its first NCAA men's Division I basketball championship. The improvements bolstered Tug. "I really felt, now, that I belonged in the Big Ten," Tug recalled.[138] The 1930s and early 1940s proved to be the a golden era for Northwestern, producing four football championships, two in basketball, one in baseball, two in swimming, three in tennis, and one in fencing.

Northwestern and Family Life

Tug's personal life during his tenure at Northwestern often overlapped with his professional duties. His family grew with the addition of two daughters; Nancy was born in 1930 and Suzanne in 1934.

Frequent trips downstate included visits to their grandparents or speaking engagements for Tug—appearances often reported on the society page of local newspapers. He rarely turned down invitations to speak to social groups or high schools, and he maintained a great rapport with news reporters throughout his career. "Sometimes he had to have fun with fledgling reporters," David Condon of the *Chicago Tribune* said. But "he treated cub reporters with the same dignity he extended the exalted."[139]

Tug also began his lifelong association with Rotary International in Evanston, the home of its national headquarters. The organization's dedication to humanitarian service and advancement of goodwill and peace around the

---

138 *The Big Ten*, 177.
139 Codon, David. 1979. "Tug Wilson Always Performed as Gold Medal Winner." *Chicago Tribune*, February 6, 1979.

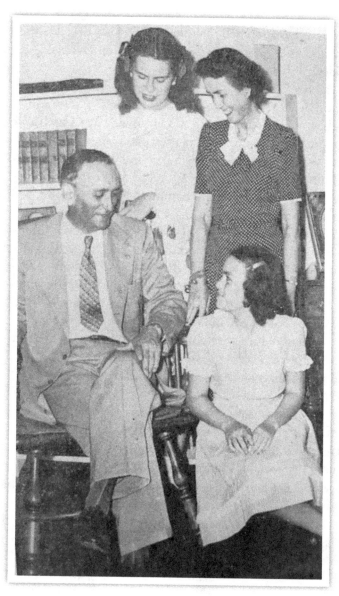

Tug with his wife, Dorothy, and their two daughters, Nancy and Suzie. Reproduced by permission of News-Gazette Media. Permission does not imply endorsement.

world fit Tug's approach to athletics. Tug also served as the youth activities director of the Office of Civil Defense and as president of his country club.

After his father died in 1934, Tug more frequently visited his mother in Atwood. He kept in touch with family and friends, enjoying reminiscing about growing up in such a small community. "Tug and I talked often about the opportunities we had as a young person growing up in our community," his cousin Bruce Carroll[140] said. "We felt that it was the ideal community, a very successful community." Tug, he said, was amazed how the community grew over the years to include a locker plant, three or four successful grocery stores, three farm-implement dealerships, and a car dealership. The school remained the center of social activities. "In the 1940s, Atwood was a thriving community," Carroll said. "He couldn't get over that. He thought that was absolutely amazing that our little community was so vibrant." Tug was proud of growing up in Atwood and didn't hesitate to give back to his hometown whenever possible, whether speaking at graduations or donating loads of used surplus athletic equipment from Northwestern.

Losing a Best Friend and Mentor

Throughout his tenure at Northwestern, Tug had never been too far from his mentor and friend, Major John Griffith, who stayed in Chicago while serving as Big Ten commissioner. Not only did Tug continue seeking his advice, but Griffith often invited him to accompany him to meetings involving Big Ten issues. Tug considered it a privilege to be "of real service to the man who had helped me get into the Big Ten."[141]

In 1929, when Tug was taking his turn as chairman of the conference directors, Griffith asked him and two other

---

140 Personal interview at Carroll's home in Savoy, Illinois, on March 5, 2019. He died October 14, 2019.
141 *The Big Ten*, 199.

veteran directors to discuss a serious violation of conference rules at the University of Iowa. Several football players there had been receiving an illegal monthly stipend from a slush fund.[142] The revelation led to the athletic director's resignation and conference officials suspending Iowa's membership and canceling its football schedule. It was the first action of its kind in athletic history. Years later, Griffith sought Tug's help in tackling the problem of big-league scouts raiding baseball college teams for players. He and Griffith also occasionally returned to Drake to help officiate the relays. Griffith met regularly with athletic directors as well as faculty representatives within the conference.

On December 7, 1944, Griffith met with both groups during a joint meeting at the Hotel Sherman in Chicago. The meeting's agenda included approving another five-year contract with Griffith, who seemed happy and in high spirits, Tug recalled. At the end of the day, Tug and L. W. St. John, the athletics director at Ohio State University, waited in the lobby, planning to accompany Griffith to dinner at the University Club of Chicago. When Griffith didn't appear, Tug went to Griffith's third-floor office. He found the door open and Griffith lying dead on the floor—the victim of an apparent heart attack. "It was a terrific shock," Tug later wrote. "He had been my best friend through the years."[143]

When he was hired as commissioner in 1922, Griffith was exactly what conference officials had been looking for to mediate school issues, investigate the eligibility of student athletes, foster relationships with students and alumni, study athletic problems, and promote fair play. The Illinois native had been a multisport athlete at Beloit College in Wisconsin, a coach at Yankton College in South Dakota and at Morningside College in Iowa, and an athletics director at

---

142 A slush fund consists of a secret cache of money used for illicit purposes.
143 *The Big Ten*, 203.

Drake. An editorial in the *Kansas City Star* had once lauded Griffith as being an "able tactician, a liberal minded non-partisan referee and finally a square dealer."[144] The 67-year-old Griffith, who had suffered ill health and a previous heart attack, had dedicated a third of his life serving the conference. Tug lauded Griffith in an official statement released after his death. "The Western Conference and intercollegiate athletics have lost their staunchest friend and greatest supporter," he wrote. Griffith was "a tower of strength at all times."[145]

Griffith had left some pretty big shoes to fill.

144 *The Kansas City Star*. 1925. "Sporting Comment." January 25, 1925, 16.
145 Jordan, Jimmy. 1944. "Griffith, Big Ten Czar, Dies: Death Follows Loop's 5-year Pact." *The Des Moines Register*, December 8, 1944.

PART 3:

Czar

Tug was named Big Ten Commissioner in 1945.

CHAPTER 11

Another Career Change

Faculty representatives asked conference athletic directors to survey the field of administrators and recommend a qualified man to succeed Griffith. In the interim, a committee comprising of Tug, St. John, and H. O. "Fritz" Crisler from the University of Michigan shared the commissioner's duties. In the early months of 1945, they had yet to receive an application from a qualified candidate and pondered the possibility of recruiting someone from inside the conference. They also secretly discussed giving the next commissioner a better salary and more power to enforce conference rules. Sports writers across the country speculated for months about who would permanently take the helm; some touted inside information about the selection. A Wisconsin sports columnist suggested Crisler or Harry Stuhldreher at the University of Wisconsin-Madison likely were the leading contenders.[146] While coaching football at Michigan, Crisler had introduced the platoon system of play—using distinct groups of players for offense and defense. The Associated Press later credited him with helping move college football from

---

146 *Wisconsin State Journal.* 1944. "Rowdy Says," December 13, 1944, newspapers.com.

a "'rah, 'rah campus pastime in the 1930s into the modern, multimillion-dollar enterprise"[147] it became. Stuhldreher, the former Notre Dame quarterback and member of the team's legendary "Four Horsemen" backfield, had coaching experience at Villanova and Wisconsin. But, Crisler "long has been boomed as the No. 1 choice for the job," according to an article in the *Iowa City Press-Citizen*.[148]

Press reports also floated the name Karl E. Leib, a professor from the University of Iowa, as a possible contender. Supporters touted his experience as a Big Ten faculty representative. Tug's name was submitted by St. John, Guy Mackey of Purdue, and Doug Mills of Illinois. Tug said he never considered pursuing the nomination, supporting Crisler instead. "He was a man who had proven himself to be a great administrator and director at Minnesota and at Michigan," Tug later wrote. "I felt he would be the perfect man to run the conference."[149] Tug told reporters he would be flattered if he was offered the post, but news accounts claiming he had an inside track for the job made him uncomfortable because of his role as interim administrator.

Tug's credentials mirrored those of Griffith's. Both had experience as an athlete, coach and administrator, and both were strong advocates of amateur athletes. Tug also had a reputation as a problem solver and negotiator who earned the respect of those involved.

Chicago Times sports editor Gene Kessler analyzed his top three picks: Tug, whom he said, "drips with personality, the kind that makes you feel at home in his company"; Army Lt. Col. Frank McCormack, a former professional baseball player known as the "boisterous type . . . who would have the Big Ten taking headlines away from major league baseball"; and former NFL coach Jimmy Conzelman, the "outside" man

147 H.O. "Fritz" Crisler. Associated Press, 1968, en.Wikipedia.com.
148 *Iowa City Press-Citizen*, Feb. 16, 1945, from newspapers.com.
149 *The Big Ten*, 207.

with a "silver tongue." Kessler predicted Tug likely would be chosen if the conference officials weren't bold enough to ignore tradition.[150]

Despite early predictions that Crisler was a cinch to win the post, those who knew him well realized the coach's deep connection with Michigan likely would keep him there. Tug's name began appearing more and more in the news as the likely heir to the throne. "If they counted the ballets today, Wilson would win in a walk," sportswriter James Enright of the *Chicago Herald-American* wrote in December.[151]

Tug never let on that he was seriously considering the position. A Western Union message Tug sent his wife on February 16 hinted that he already had been offered the job. Dorothy and Tug had been exchanging telegrams while she visited in Tucson, Arizona. He wanted his wife's opinion again on making another important career move. Dorothy thought it was a great offer and a wonderful opportunity, telling her husband she hoped he would accept.[152] "Got your sweet wire and shortly after job landed in my lap," he wrote in the telegram. "Keep it quiet," he added.[153] Tug met with the faculty board all day on Friday, March 9, and expected a final vote later that day. However, the absence of one board member forced a delay. "Appointment delayed until Sat but ok in every way," Tug wired to his wife. "Cold better. Children swell. Got your letter just at right time. All my love."[154]

Tug officially became the second commissioner in Big Ten history by a unanimous vote. In a letter he wrote Dorothy that weekend, Tug revealed his six-year contract with the Big

150 Kessler, Gene. 1944. "2 Standouts for Big 10 Post." *Chicago Tribune*, Undated clipping from Atwood-Hammond Public Library collection.
151 Enright, James. *Chicago Herald-American*, December 30, 1944.
152 *The Big Ten*, 208.
153 Actual Western Union telegram sent February 16, 1945, is part of the Tug Wilson collection at the Atwood-Hammond Public Library.
154 Actual Western Union telegram sent March 9, 1945, is part of the Tug Wilson collection at the Atwood-Hammond Public Library.

Ten included a $15,000 salary with a $500 raise each of the next five years, a stipulation to fund his retirement, and a "very liberal" expense account of $2,000. The board, however, insisted he quit his job with the Chicago school system. "I did reluctantly but there was nothing else to do," he told her.[155] Tug's compensation package differed greatly from Griffith's, who earned $10,000 salary with a $500 expense account.

News of the appointment hit publications across the country, especially in those states within the Big Ten. "Wilson is chosen as Commissioner of Big Ten Sports" read a headline in the *New York Times*. "BIG TEN NAMES TUG WILSON COMMISSIONER," the *Chicago Sunday Tribune* announced. "I intend to give the office my full time and attention and to build on the marvelous foundation left by Major Griffith," Tug told the press.[156] He was set to take office on May 1, 1945, giving Tug time to help Northwestern during the transition. "I have enjoyed my work there and the thought of leaving at this time is the only regret I have," he wrote.

Northwestern officials characterized Tug's appointment as "merited recognition" but also found it difficult to tell him goodbye after two decades. "Mr. Wilson has made many lasting contributions to Northwestern University athletics," President Franklyn Bliss Snyder told reporters. "We like him and will find it hard to get along without him."[157]

Days after the appointment, the *St. Louis Globe-Democrat* reported Tug may not have been the conference's first choice. "Crisler, it was learned, turned down the offer and backed Wilson for the job," according to the article.[158] A brief sentence

---

155 Actual letter written by Tug on March 10, 1945, and is part of the Tug Wilson collection at the Atwood-Hammond Public Library.

156 Taken from actual handwritten note and part of the Tug Wilson collection at the Atwood-Hammond Public Library.

157 Prell, Edward. 1945. "Maj. Griffith's Successor to Start May 1." *Chicago Tribune*, March 11, 1945, 27.

158 Associated Press, *St. Louis Globe-Democrat*. 1945. "Tug Wilson Appointed Big Ten Commissioner." March 11, 1945, 19.

in Tug's March 10 letter to his wife appears to have confirmed that report. "The contract is even better than Fritz . . . *(sic)*," he wrote. Tug wrote decades later that Crisler did not want the position because he had been "happily situated" at Michigan.[159]

Notes of congratulations trickled in for months. Tug even received a message from the Brisbane Illini Club in Australia in June. Chili Bowen (class of 1935) wrote the note on rice paper taken from a Japanese soldier. "Good luck in your new venture Tug. They couldn't have selected a more popular Wildcat Brave," he said.[160]

The changing of the conference guard created an opportunity for faculty representatives to reconsider the commissioner's role. Before the conference was formed, there were no eligibility rules. Players, known as tramp athletes, could participate in one sport at a school one season and another sport at a different school the same year; or play at one school one year and move to another the next year without penalty. It also was common to see tramp coaches, or for coaches to play on their own teams, for professional athletes to play on collegiate teams, and for players to be paid.

The new faculty committee put an end to those practices, adopting some basic rules requiring all players to be bona fide students working toward a degree. Although Griffith had been hired to assist the committee in ensuring compliance, they considered him a "general secretary"[161] with no authority to enforce the rules. That role often meant Griffith collected information and then presented it to the athletic directors and faculty board for possible action. When he learned alumni at some member schools made illegal offers to players, for example, all Griffith could do was create a program to educate

159 *The Big Ten*, 207.
160 Actual letter kept and is part of the Tug Wilson collection at the Atwood-Hammond Public Library.
161 *The Big Ten*, 190.

them about the rules. Tug would have the power Griffith didn't have. The committee now allowed the commissioner to interpret and rule upon conference regulations,

Sports writers titled the new role as a "czar," a word Tug despised. "The commissioner is still an executive agent of both the athletic directors and the faculty representatives," he insisted. "It is in no sense a czar or dictator and I certainly have no such ideas."[162]

It may have appeared to some that Tug, now forty-nine, rode on Griffith's coattails from Illinois to Iowa, then to Northwestern to the Big Ten. For the most part, though, it was Griffith who opened the door. Tug earned his reputation as an honorable, hardworking professional and was smart enough to seize the opportunities afforded him. While at Northwestern, Tug served on the Olympic track and field committee, worked with the NCAA's Olympic committee, and attended the Olympics in 1924, 1928, and 1932. He also succeeded Griffith as secretary-treasurer of the NCAA. His involvement in various organizations dedicated to amateur athletics required meeting with like minds around the country. As commissioner, Tug worked with member schools but also represented the conference in the NCAA, an organization created in 1906 to regulate collegiate sports in the United States.

---

162 Wilson's handwritten official statement to press upon being named commissioner.

"Wilson is chosen as Commissioner of Big Ten Sports"

Headline in the *New York Times*.

1947 Rose Bowl program cover

CHAPTER 12

Integrity of the Game

As commissioner, Tug believed maintaining a trustworthy and educated team of game officials was important to ensuring the integrity within the Big Ten. One of the greatest dangers? Gambling. Betting on sporting events invited corruption among officials, coaches, and even players. With enough cash, gamblers could pay off those people who had the power to affect a game's outcome. "It [gambling] must be curbed despite the urge of the American public to wager on the outcome of sports events," he said.[163]

Tug witnessed the extent of gambling's popularity while on a college trip to Columbus to watch the Illini take on Ohio State. In the lobby of his hotel, Tug saw a betting frenzy with thousands of dollars on a table being guarded by police. "I felt tremendously troubled by what I'd witnessed, and I thought it significant when a vigorous campaign was initiated the following year to end this kind of blatant betting on college games." [164] As commissioner, Tug made it a rule never to hire a game official unless the applicant's business or professional work was carefully investigated

163 Enright, James. 1951. "Wilson Hits 'Pressure' on Grid." *Chicago Herald-American*, October 9, 1951.
164 *The Big Ten*, 137.

for potential conflicts of interest. He assigned people to observe officials during games and submit a written report to his office. Members of the officiating staff were required to attend regular meetings and pass rule examinations.

Basketball especially faced close scrutiny for any evidence of point-fixing or point-shaving—an intentional effort to control scoring to maintain the margin of victory. As precautionary measures, Tug required players to report anyone who approached them about point-fixing and expected coaches to restrict telephone calls to hotel rooms before a game; he urged coaches and players to not discuss team injuries and exhorted officials to not discuss teams or players with anyone. Conference officials also monitored major odds-making centers for sudden shifts and watched games for an unusual number of foul calls.

Suspected violators faced "stiff interrogations" at times. Although some of those reports were inconclusive, other investigations determined there was enough evidence to ask for the officials' immediate resignation. "All this was quite distasteful to me, but I can say that Big Ten players and officials came through the era without scandals," he said.[165]

Thorny Problems at the Tournament of Roses

Tug inherited several unresolved conference projects when he took office, and it didn't take long for him to tackle one of the most exciting—pursuing an exclusive agreement with the Pacific Coast Conference (PCC). For years, officials with the California-based organization had

---

165 *The Big Ten*, 235. The University of Illinois self-reported recruiting violations to the Big Ten, admitting to paying players from 1962 to 1966 from a slush fund. Illinois fired football coach Pete Elliott, basketball coach Harry Combe, and assistant basketball coach Howie Braun under threat of the school being expelled from the conference.

been inviting the Big Ten to send its best team to play in the Rose Bowl in Pasadena. The bowl, played on New Year's Day, was created to help fund the city's annual parade, started in 1890. The parade attracted thousands of visitors who lined the city streets to watch the elaborate, flower-covered floats as well as bands and equestrian units. Hoping to attract larger crowds, organizers added a football game in 1902, pitting the best team from the East against the best team in the West. The first Tournament of Roses (later known as the Rose Bowl) ended with Michigan defeating Stanford, 49–0: a blowout that didn't help create much excitement. For the next fourteen years, organizers tried polo matches, greased pig catches, tug-of-war competitions, ostrich races, and even chariot races, but finally realized football had the mass appeal they wanted.

Football returned in 1916 with Washington State University defeating Brown University, 14–0: still a blowout, but popular. Growing attendance prompted officials to build a new stadium, dedicated in 1922, with a seating capacity of over 90,000. To this day, it remains one of the largest stadiums in the country and the world. No Big Ten team appeared at the Tournament of Roses from 1916 to 1921 because Big Ten directors and faculty representatives had barred any member teams from postseason play. The majority believed the season already was too long and that schools put too much emphasis on football. Griffith supported a change and had been entertaining discussions on the subject for at least eight years prior to his death.

Tug and his staff began researching the objections and opened negotiations with their Pacific Coast counterparts. One concern was that players would miss too many classes. Information presented to the Big Ten faculty representatives, however, showed that football players had fewer recorded absences than athletes in other sports. Tug intended to keep it that way. Under the proposed pact presented in late 1946, the

Big Ten Conference winner would play in the Rose Bowl, but no conference team could go two consecutive years. This prevented one team from monopolizing the game by a long winning streak. The pact also required conference proceeds to be divided equally—a plan later adopted by other conferences.

Tug credited his staff for ironing out all the details of the agreement, which met with general acceptance barring a few exceptions. The Pacific Coast Conference didn't like the no-repeat provision because it wanted the Big Ten champion every year. The PCC members also were adamant the pact didn't begin until the 1947 season because they wanted to invite Army, not conference champion Illinois, to participate in the Rose Bowl at the end of the 1946 season.

Sports writers on the coast weren't enthusiastic either. They wanted the eleventh-ranked Cadets to play. Until that season, Army had a twenty-three-game unbeaten streak dating to1944. Pact opponents, however, didn't like Army's reputation for recruiting the best college players from the Big Ten. After a twenty-four-hour debate, Big Ten representatives ratified a five-year agreement on September 1, 1946.[166] The *Los Angeles Evening Citizen News* broke the news with the headline: "PCC, Big Nine Shut Out Army in Five-Year Pact."

The first Rose Bowl under the new agreement pitted the University of California, Los Angeles, against the Fighting Illini. Critical California sportswriters weren't shy

---

166 From the Big Ten, Illinois and Wisconsin voted against the pact. In the PCC, UCLA and USC voted against the pact. The PCC/Western Conference agreement was continually renewed until 1959 when the PCC was dissolved following a pay-for-play scandal the year before. The PCC was reorganized as the Athletic Association of Western Universities and selected a Rose Bowl representative in 1960. It later was renamed the Pac-10. The two conferences played without an agreement until 1963. The exclusive agreement between the two conferences lasted until the Bowl Championship Series was introduced in 1998.

about expressing their feelings about Illinois, a team they considered "second-rate."[167] Tug came head-to-head with that sentiment while preparing to speak at the Los Angeles Times Sports Award Dinner. The crowd booed him when he was introduced. Tug stood his ground, defended the Illini, and even predicted they would win. He was correct. The Fighting Illini defeated UCLA 45–14 before a crowd of over 93,000 fans. To add insult to injury, Big Ten teams dominated the PCC at the Rose Bowl with a 12–1 winning record until 1960.[168]

---

167 *The Big Ten*, 230.
168 Rose Bowl (Tournament of Roses) Game Results, Los Angeles Almanac, LaAlmanac.com.

Televised sports did not exist when Tug (right)
played football at the University of Illinois. But as
Big Ten commissioner, he helped usher in the era
of televised collegiate sports. (University of Illinois)

CHAPTER 13

The Big Ten and the Golden Age of Television

The Rose Bowl has been known as the "granddaddy" of all bowl games because it is the oldest and considered the most prestigious. The annual contest showed the sports world the value of combining tourism-rich regional festivals with college football games.

The 1930s gave rise to four other "bowls": the Sugar Bowl, the Cotton Bowl Classic, the Orange Bowl, and the Sun Bowl. Universities had capitalized on accommodating larger crowds, but they also realized the financial importance of participating in a bowl game. The number of bowls subsequently continued to rise nearly every decade. Enter television.

The Rose Bowl was first televised in 1947 on W6XYZ, an experimental station later known as KTLA, and came at the beginning of the Golden Age of Television. Football fans who could afford a receiver now could watch games from the comfort of their homes—a phenomenon that worried Tug and the Big Ten schools. When radio began broadcasting sporting events in the 1920s, universities predicted lower attendance and, thus, lower gate receipts. To Tug's surprise, the advent of radio actually increased interest in football and other sports. Television, however, was a different matter, especially for small colleges that feared fans would rather sit at home and watch the "big" college games or the increasingly prevalent professional football games. In an interview with *Billboard*[169] in 1951, Tug said a study of gate receipts when the University of Michigan began televising its games, showed attendance dropped, on average, from 11,000 to 600 per game. "We may find TV isn't the menace it is said to be, but all our evidence is to the contrary," he said in the article. "We're not dumb enough to say to television 'Get out. You're hurting us. We can't get along with you.'"

The NCAA needed a plan to protect the small schools while spreading financial benefit to different areas. Broadcast executives, willing to pay generously for exclusive rights, knew the best competitions attracted the most viewers, increased their ratings and ultimately maximized their advertising revenue. In 1950, Pennsylvania State and Notre Dame signed individual five-year contracts to broadcast their games regionally—an agreement that brought $150,000 into Penn State's coffers.

In the Big Ten, televised games played on home grounds were prohibited. Instead, game films were available for postseason telecasts, but that didn't satisfy television stations that wanted timely games to show their viewers. Determined to protect game attendance, the NCAA asserted control in 1951 and prohibited live broadcasts. It wasn't a popular decision, and it forced Penn State and Notre Dame to break their contracts. The NCAA responded to threats of antitrust lawsuits by lifting blackouts of certain sold-out games. The next year, NCAA officials limited live coverage to a weekly game and sold exclusive broadcast rights for more than $1.1 million.

Tug recalls the Big Ten received tempting offers for exclusive broadcast rights to conference games, but to do so

---

169 *Billboard*, via newspapers.com.

meant losing NCAA membership. For him, it wasn't worth it. He was, however, unhappy with the weekly game plan and pressured the NCAA to allow regional telecasts as well. Tug worked with the NCAA to limit the number of games in which a school might appear and to prohibit televised games if there were other small college games in that vicinity at the same time. Small colleges also avoided conflict by moving their games to Friday nights. In 1955, the NCAA revised its rules again, keeping eight nationally televised games while permitting true regional telecasts during five weeks of the football season. The organization's plan also called for pooling all football television rights and sharing proceeds equally.

Tug Wilson, center, is surrounded by George Halas,
Red Grange, Bob Richards, Lou Boudreau, and
Thomas Dwight "Dike" Eddleman.

CHAPTER 14

Raising a Crop
of Wholesome Athletes

For Tug, helping to create an enviable postseason event was one of the most exciting aspects of being commissioner. On the flip side, however, he encountered problems that sometimes required him to make necessary but unpopular decisions. The end of World War II brought students back to college, thanks to the Servicemen's Readjustment Act of 1944—better known as the G.I. Bill. The legislation paid tuition and fees for 2.2 million returning veterans looking to continue their education.[170] After World War I, most veterans returned to schools near their hometowns. World War II veterans proved to be different, spreading out all over the country. That posed eligibility issues, especially for those returning athletes whose collegiate careers had been interrupted by serving their country.

Officials had relaxed many of the conference rules during wartime, even lifting the ban on freshmen playing on varsity teams. The decision to revert to prewar rules, however, caused dissension among the ranks. Some athletic directors wanted to continue allowing freshmen to play because it gave coaches

---

170 https://en.wikipedia.org/wiki/G.I._Bill.

more depth on their team while giving the player more experience. Although Tug conceded that freshmen could benefit from a limited amount of competition, he believed requiring them to complete at least a semester first gave them an incentive to maintain good grades. From the influx of veterans, Tug also predicted the expansion of intramural sports, creating the era of building new field houses and indoor facilities. To meet the growing needs, Tug and some coaches advocated creating "B teams" to accommodate more participants, especially for those strong "150-pounders" who could not make varsity squads. "Maybe those lightweights won't be able to crowd 200-pounders off the varsity," he told reporters. "But I think it's the job of athletics administrators to see that they get a chance to compete to their heart's content in regular fashion."[171]

Efforts to Enforce the Rules and Cleanup Sports

Tug believed a commissioner's job as an athletic administrator required keeping a watchful eye for excesses that crept into college sports and taking decisive action against those who broke the rules. He recognized the pitfalls competitive sports naturally created, but he insisted the desire to win should never outweigh the importance of getting a good education. "Any commissioner worth his salt must deal with an iron hand," he said, while also advocating uniform adherence to the rules.[172] His efforts to "clean up" the conference began with general investigations that uncovered some inconsistencies. At two schools, he discovered students could remove a failing grade by taking an exam—a popular choice among affected top athletes. "It was like getting a second turn at bat after you had struck

---

171 *Chicago Tribune*. 1945. "'B' Grid for Ex G. Is Wilson Aim." May 1, 1945.
172 *The Big Ten*, 246.

out," Tug argued.[173] The conference banned the practice in 1947.

Tug also found a number of Big Ten athletes received money from alumni or sports fans, a definite no-no, which cost those athletes one year of eligibility. "Penalties of this kind were very painful to me," Tug admitted.[174]

He tracked the progress of about a dozen of those athletes and found that after one year, few remained in college. One coach found to have illegally recruited was banned from recruiting altogether for one year.

Recruiting and financial-assistance issues provided Tug and his staff with a "constant headache,"[175] requiring long and tedious investigations. Lacking the power to issue subpoenas, investigators could not force witnesses to answer questions under oath. Tug often encountered sharp businessmen who "seemed to regard this as just a game"[176] and were good at covering their tracks. "Many times I grew disgusted at my inability to get the job done," he recalled.[177] With the faculty board's blessing, Tug hired Jack Ryan, a former conference athlete and FBI agent, who had been working as a private investigator. Ryan's job, along with other investigators employed as needed, was to help the commissioner gather information about alleged infractions. "He will not be a Gestapo agent," Tug told a joint meeting with directors and the faculty board. "He will seek only the facts that are necessary to enforce confidence in the integrity of our program."[178]

Two of the most important rules adopted in 1949 addressed player compensation and unearned financial aid.

---

173 *The Big Ten*, 232.
174 *The Big Ten*, 257.
175 *The Big Ten*, 242.
176 *The Big Ten*, 273.
177 *The Big Ten*, 273.
178 *Star Tribune (Minneapolis, Minnesota)*. 1955. "Big-Ten Hires Ex-FBI Agent." June 12, 1955, 39.

- Rule #6: No student could be declared eligible to play if he has ever used his knowledge of or skill in athletics for financial gain; taken part in an athletic contest in which a money prize was offered; gave his name to any form of commercial advertising; and received compensation from any employer unless the work performed is useful, pays the going rate, and the requires the student to be on the job for the duration of the time he is paid.

- Rule #7: No player could receive at any time other than from persons to whom he is naturally or legally dependent, unless he qualifies either by superior scholarship or demonstrated need. Any qualified assistance could not exceed the tuition and incidental fees charged by the university. The rule also required incoming freshmen to rank in the upper half of his graduating class or have scored above the 50th percentile on an entrance exam or standard college aptitude examination. Transfer students must have achieved a grade point average no lower than one-fourth of the way between "C" and "B" grades.

The governing board also adopted what was known as the "Sanity Code," designed to take a sane and direct approach to the problem of administrating legitimate athletic aid. The code required all aid to be administered by a university's scholarship committee. Tug made sure the rules were well publicized, printing them in alumni magazines, posting copies in locker rooms, and briefing coaches about what they could and could not do.

Conference officials tightened rules governing unearned aid again in 1952. Under these regulations, schools could not grant scholarship aid unless the prospective student obtained superior academic standing (defined as being in the upper third of his graduation class) and made quantitative progress toward a degree. That didn't bother excellent scholar athletes, but it was a problem[179] for a majority of athletes who didn't graduate even in the top half of their high school class. Those athletes who couldn't qualify for a scholarship worked a summer job and returned to school to likely wait tables at their fraternity or perform other odd jobs in order to pay their own way. "My hat is off to those who made it, and many did, in doing so received the valuable training of learning to budget their time," Tug said. [180]

But the commissioner found that many athletes could not make it and either flunked out or quietly withdrew to reenter neighboring conferences that didn't have academic requirements for scholarships. "The attrition of Big Ten freshmen athletes became quite alarming," he said.[181] The rules obviously placed an almost impossible burden on athletes, and yet the conference stuck to this program through the mid-1950s. Tug quietly created a special committee to study overall problems within the conference—a self-evaluation of conduct involving intercollegiate athletics.[182]

Flexing Muscle

Tug's first serious test of his enforcement power came in 1953. When Michigan State College (later known as Michigan State University) joined the Big Ten in 1949, it agreed to accept all conference rules and gave up its athletic scholarship program permissible under NCAA rules, but not the conference rules. Tug's office began receiving complaints against the school, claiming an organization known as the Spartan Foundation was giving athletes unearned aid. The foundation's president refused to release information about the

---

179 *The Big Ten*, 296.
180 *The Big Ten*, 296.
181 *The Big Ten*, 296.
182 The committee was comprised of Tug; his assistant, Bill Reed; Crisler; Leslie Scott, a Michigan faculty representative; Verne C. Freeman of Purdue; and Ivy Williamson, athletic director at Wisconsin.

fund or how it operated, claiming it had no connection with Michigan State.

In February of that year, Tug notified university president Dr. John Hannah after the foundation failed to respond to a second request. Through Hannah, officials turned over $2,000 to the Michigan State scholarship fund and agreed they would process all future scholarships through college channels. State records showed the foundation reported $38,209 in assets and had dispersed about $17,500 in 1951, including funds to athletes, band members, and nonathletic upperclassmen who were having financial difficulties.[183] The fund, Tug determined, was operated entirely without the knowledge of athletic department staff. On May 27, 1952, Tug placed Michigan State on probation for one year—the first time in athletic history an institution of this size had been punished for violating the rules. The school had one year to correct the problem or face possible expulsion from the conference.

Hannah appealed, claiming it was impossible for the school to police thousands of alumni and friends in their recruiting and subsidizing activities—an issue that concerned many other college presidents. He also argued conference rules did not specifically grant the commissioner the right to assess the punishment. Faculty representatives rejected the arguments and upheld the penalty.[184] Probation, Tug later wrote, was a "fair and just" punishment that became a standard practice not only in the conference, but with the NCAA as well. "Frankly, it was one of the most significant actions taken by the Big Ten since the Conference had been formed," he later noted.[185]

---

183 *The Big Ten*, 278-279.
184 In 1951, the faculty representatives reorganized the rules clearly defining the jurisdiction of the reps and athletics directors. Conference legislation also established the commissioner as the primary enforcement agent and clearly defined his duties.
185 *The Big Ten*, 284.

Where There's Smoke, There's Usually Fire

Information about possible rule violations came from a variety of sources. Sometimes it was rumors or questions from sports writers that alerted Tug; other times it was a tip from a coach eager to blow the whistle on a rival. Subsequent investigations often revealed unfounded accusations—a problem that forced faculty representatives to adopt a rule requiring alleged violations be reported to the faculty rep and athletic director, not the press. Of course, not every complaint could be investigated. Tug just didn't have enough staff members. Usually, he waited until his office received a substantial number of complaints that seemed to fit into a pattern. "To use the old adage, 'where you have smoke, you usually find fire,'" he said.[186]

Tug resolved other questionable practices: he barred prospective athletes from playing a scrimmage involving any of the school's varsity players, which constituted a tryout; he ruled college-sponsored summer camps are allowed if the high school athlete paid his full camp fee; and he required a conference athlete playing baseball in a summer league to submit a statement from the team manager verifying the athlete was not receiving a share of the gate receipts or cash prize.

A bigger issue surfaced involving college work programs where many athletes earned the extra money they needed to continue college. Tug didn't see a problem with student athletes contributing to their college expenses, believing the students benefited from the experience. However, the commissioner began receiving a considerable number of complaints questioning the validity of these jobs and if the athletes were actually working. Tug's inquiries led him to Ohio State University, which offered athletes state house jobs in Columbus and jobs at hotels and other businesses. The

---

186 *The Big Ten*, 277.

jobs offered athletes an opportunity to work sixteen hours per week for $50 to $75 a month. If the student couldn't fulfill the time requirement, he could make up the time during the off-season but still receive full pay in the meantime—a violation of conference rules.

A *Sports Illustrated* article published in 1955[187] also revealed that Ohio football coach Woody Hayes often used his personal funds to help players in need. Hayes admitted he sometimes helped players in "dire distress,"[188] loaning them money to avoid eviction or to pay bus fare home. Without his help, the coach told Tug, some players may have dropped out of school. Tug noted, however, Hayes didn't maintain a written record of these "loans." On April 26, 1956, the commissioner placed Ohio State University on probation for one year. During that time, the school could not participate in the Rose Bowl and was required to complete job records and obtain a full disclosure of Hayes's loans. Ohio athletes also would not be deemed eligible to play unless they made up the work or they could prove they actually had worked. Tug praised Ohio State officials for meeting all the requirements. To do that, a number of athletes worked their entire spring break and part of the summer to make up any deficits. The Ohio State investigation showed how impractical and unrealistic a work program had become. As Tug pointed out, there just weren't enough hours in a day for an athlete to meet all his college expenses.

Threats to Intercollegiate Sports

Four months after assessing the Ohio State ruling, Tug's special committee released a critical twenty-four-page report concluding work-aid rules were being "bent, if not tortured" throughout the conference thus inviting "hypocrisy and deceit"[189]

---

187 *Sports Illustrated.* 1955. "The Ohio State Story." October 24, 1955.
188 *The Big Ten,* 291.
189 Associated Press, *Kansas City Times.* 1956. "Big Ten Eyes Monster." October 16, 1956, 23.

if left unchecked. The investigation found earned and unearned financial subsidies had increased in "staggering proportions" in the past decade, from $56,694 in 1948 to $348,688 in 1955. The strongly worded report predicted intercollegiate sports would become nothing more than "farms" where athletes build personal nest eggs with financial aid funds while creating "virtual anarchy" in administrating the rules and regulations and killing non-revenue-producing sports and intramurals. "The distinction between intercollegiate sports and professional sports will become so invisible that public support will shift to the latter," according to the report. "The resulting financial chaos will force the abandonment of the intercollegiate system."[190] The report was supposed to have been distributed only to Big Ten presidents, athletic directors, and faculty representatives, but somehow it was leaked to the press.

Just a week before the release, Tug discussed rule enforcement during a joint meeting between members of the Football Coaches Association and the Football Writers Association in Chicago. The commissioner compared attempts to enforce the rules governing collegiate athletes to the Prohibition of 1920–1933 when federal authorities attempted to enforce the alcohol ban that most Americans didn't support and fought to circumvent. "I think we've got to come back to institutional integrity," Tug said about collegiate athletics. "And until we, as conferences and as leaders in our field, believe in the rules, they will never be given the right enforcement."[191]

Indiana Hoosier's Controversy

Indiana University was at a disadvantage when attempting to recruit football players in a state where high schools

---

190 Associated Press, *Kansas City Times*. 1956. "Big Ten Eyes Monster." October 16, 1956, 23.

191 Johnson, Raymond. 1956. "One Man's Opinion." *The Tennessean*, August 14, 1956, 16.

preferred basketball. During a time in the 1950s, only fifty-nine high schools fielded a football team. After the Hoosiers ended at the bottom of the conference in 1956, officials hired Phil Dickens, hoping to rebuild a program worthy of the new stadium and field house being planned. It appeared Indiana was on the horizon of a new era in football. But it wasn't in the way the Hoosiers expected.

Tug soon heard Indiana was making "fantastic"[192] offers of financial assistance, above and beyond the normal student expenses. A number of individual athletes confirmed they had met with Dickens privately in his office and were told the university would pay their room, books, tuition, meals, and fifty dollars a month for expenses. On July 18, 1957, Tug notified Herman Wells, the president of Indiana University, and within weeks university officials and Dickens promised 100 percent compliance. The faculty representatives suspended Dickens from all coaching duties for one year but agreed to reinstate him in December that year.

Tug quietly continued investigating the reported irregularities during the probation period and for the next two years. What he found astonished him. A few freshmen prospects in 1957 to 1959 admitted being offered or having received illegal financial assistance. One group that had enrolled, but later flunked out, reported receiving monthly payments in plain envelopes placed in their campus mailboxes. The investigation also found a younger coach, hired in 1958, registered under an assumed name during recruiting trips, apparently to ensure hotel clerks couldn't inform local colleges that a recruiter was in town. His other tactics involved working with alumni who would make illegal offers when the coach left the room.

---

192 *The Big Ten*, 300.

And then there were reports from prospective recruits in Ohio and West Virginia who said they received a telephone call from a "Mr. Palmer" who claimed to be an Indiana alumnus from Kentucky. During the conversation, the man told each boy he would receive fifty dollars a month and a round-trip airfare at Christmas and Thanksgiving if they signed with Indiana. The young coach made the mistake of being introduced as Palmer during one recruiting trip, an action that led to the coach's resignation.

The final nail to Indiana's coffin came from an athlete who had transferred from West Point Military Academy. In a letter to the commissioner, the athlete admitted he had accepted illegal help and was reporting it because he had become "disgusted with the whole setup and wanted to help clear up the situation."[193] Wells and the board of directors dismissed the claim, alleging it was nothing more than an attempt to discredit the school by a disgruntled athlete. But when the athlete passed a lie detector test, Tug felt compelled to take drastic action. Although Tug believed University friends or alumni had committed the infractions, he admitted he couldn't prove the University itself had been involved. "I must say, however, that I have grave doubts that any such practices on the scale suggested by the cases at hand could possibly have been carried on without the knowledge of and, indeed, the approval of the football coaching staff,"[194] Tug wrote in a letter to Wells.

As a penalty, Indiana University was placed on probation for the 1960 academic year, during which the school would not receive its share of football television receipts or be counted in the conference standings. The direct loss to Indiana included nearly $100,000. Indirectly, it gave Indiana a bad image affecting recruitment. Hoosier

---

193 *The Big Ten*, 312.
194 *The Big Ten*, 313.

fans, especially Indiana students, were bitter. Tug received numerous protest letters and was even hanged in effigy from a campus tree.

The hole Indiana found itself in grew deeper. NCAA regulators placed Indiana on probation for four years, forbade televised games, and, worst of all, declared *all* Hoosier athletic teams ineligible for NCAA championship competition during the probation period. Tug felt the last stipulation was "extremely hard"[195] considering his investigation pinpointed violations only in the football program. "It's a dad-burned shame," coach Dickens told reporters. "We thought we had done everything possible to avoid anything like this. I can honestly say that neither I nor any member of my staff have ever made any offer of any kind to any boy or had any knowledge of such offer. This is the Gospel truth."[196]

Tug asked NCAA officials not to punish all teams for the errors of one, but officials stood firm, contending some violations occurred while Indiana already was on probation. The *Palladium-Item* in Richmond, Indiana, reported the sanction was "one of the most severe penalties ever imposed on a member of the NCAA." Critics put some of the blame on alumni or claimed Indiana was being used as a scapegoat. They claim the university was unfairly treated, alleging similar violations at other Big Ten universities. "I was quite upset," Indiana Governor Herold Handley said about the probation ruling. "I could single out a couple of other universities in good instances that I know about."[197]

Wells took it on the chin, vowing to make things right. "All we can do is carry on and do everything possible to

195 *The Big Ten*, 315.
196 *Chicago Tribune*. 1960. "Tug Mum on Big 10 Phase of I.U. Probe." April 28, 1960, 55.
197 Associated Press, *Palladium-Item* (Richmond, Indiana). 1960. "Former Net Coach Appointed by IU To Check On Recruiting." August 2, 1960, 8.

obtain removal as soon as possible of the cloud under which we must proceed."[198]

As much as it hurt Tug to see Indiana University suffer the consequences, he embraced the need to do what he could as commissioner to address a long-standing problem in collegiate sports. "The sentence is severe," Tug told a reporter. "I hope it has enough impact for overzealous alumni to stop and consider."[199]

Retirement as Big Ten Commissioner

March 27, 1961, marked Tug's sixty-fifth birthday—the age of mandatory retirement after serving sixteen years as Big Ten commissioner. During his final meeting with faculty representatives and athletic directors, Tug told the audience he was leaving office with deep appreciation knowing the conference had rules it could believe in and live with. "I firmly believe the athletic programs of any university will be only as honest as the integrity of the athletic director and his staff."[200] Tug also was the guest of honor at a testimonial dinner at the Delta Upsilon fraternity in Champagne-Urbana where he reminisced with his high school coach Thomas Samuels,[201] a Decatur lawyer; a former student; and former Illini teammates, Burt Ingwersen and Harold Osborn. Big Ten directors appointed former assistant Bill Reed to succeed Tug, who said he would now take a more active role in the US Olympic Committee. "I don't feel I'm exactly leaving the Big Ten because I'll be there ready to offer my experience and counsel if my successor wants," Tug said.[202]

---

198 Associated Press, *Journal & Courier* (Lafayette, Indiana). 1960. "There is No Appeal, No, Recourse: Wells." April 28, 1960, 39.
199 United Press International, *The Herald* (Jasper, Indiana). 1960. "Big Ten Take Disciplinary Action Against IU." August 1, 1960, 10.
200 *The Big Ten*, 335.
201 Samuels died in 1989 at the age of 103.
202 Associated Press, *Las Cruces Sun-News* (Las Cruces, New Mexico), 1961. "Wilson Retires as Big Ten Head, Pledges Counsel to Successor." July 2, 1961, 12.

The *Chicago Tribune* jokingly suggested the possibility of Tug returning to tilling the earth, since he "considered himself a farmer at heart." "But nothing he can raise on the farm will match the crop of wholesome athletes and good citizens which he has helped produce in the last 40 years," according to the article. "There is a crop that will never be over produced."[203]

Tug (right) and his former high school coach, Tom Samuels (left), during a retirement party in 1961. Reproduced by permission of News-Gazette Media. Permission does not imply endorsement.

_____

203 *Chicago Tribune*. 1961. "Tug Wilson Retires." May 20, 1961, 15.

PART 4:

Coming
Full
Circle

Art Devlin, ski jumper; Tenley Albright, figure skater; Tug Wilson, president of the US Olympic Committee; and Hayes Alan Jenkins, figure skater; on their way to the 1956 Winter Olympics in Cortina d'Ampezzo, Italy

CHAPTER 15

President of the USOC

In 1953, the fifty-seven-year-old Tug accepted another important position in amateur sports—president of the US Olympic Committee (USOC). He succeeded Avery Brundage[204] who resigned after twenty-five years at the helm to focus on being president of the International Olympic Committee (IOC). Brundage and Tug shared some common history and ideals but were quite opposites when it came to personality and management styles. Brundage, like Tug, graduated from the University of Illinois and competed in the Olympics. He also was a zealous advocate of amateurism, fighting against commercialization and politicization of the games. Brundage, however, was a multimillionaire who earned his fortune in the construction business. As the USOC president, he ruled with an iron fist and had a tendency to punish athletes for minor infractions of stringent rules. Brundage "did more to set the tone of the modern Olympic Games than any other individual,"[205] all the while

204 Brundage was appointed president of the IOC in 1954 and is the only American to ever hold this position. He is best known for two controversial issues: as president of the USOC he opposed boycotting the 1936 Olympics in Germany; in 1972 as president of the IOC, he declared the Olympic Games in Munich to continue despite a terrorist attack that killed eleven Israeli athletes.
205 "Avery Brundage: American Sports Administrator." Britannica.com.

developing a reputation as being domineering, racist, sexist, and anti-Semitic. Going against public opinion didn't bother Brundage, who enjoyed the limelight. Tug's reputation, on the other hand, exuded friendship, goodwill, compromise, and negotiation. He learned a round of golf often was the best strategy for resolving differences between two groups. And although he treated members of the media with respect, he didn't seek public attention.

Olympic Ideology and American Reality

Pulling double duty was especially difficult for Tug from 1955 to 1960, handling the Ohio State and Indiana investigations as the Big Ten commissioner while also preparing for two Olympiads.[206] By the time he retired from the Big Ten in 1961, Tug had led the contingent of US athletes at four Olympics: the Winter Games in Cortina d'Ampezzo, Italy, and the Summer Games in Melbourne, Australia, in 1956; and the Winter Games in Squaw Valley, California, and the Summer Games in Rome, Italy, in 1960. Tug enjoyed the competitions but insisted the Olympics taught athletes more than just how to compete. "There is no place where the lessons of good citizenship and decent behavior can be taught as well as on the athletic field and properly applied on an international level, these principles could restore peace to the world," he once told Rotarians at a luncheon in Madison, Wisconsin.[207]

Tug wholeheartedly believed in the Olympic ideals of balancing mind and body, friendship, mutual understanding, and fair play in competition free of political conflict—attributes with roots grounded deep in ancient Greece and the first recorded games conducted in 776 B.C. The

---

206 During this period, the winter and summer Olympics were conducted the same year every four years. That changed after 1992, when Olympics were held in alternate two-year intervals.

207 Cantwell, Roger. 1954. "Tug Wilson Sees Athletic Field as One of Keys to World Peace." *Wisconsin State Journal*, April 8, 1954, 28.

games were held every four years until 393 A.D. when Emperor Theodosius, a Christian, banned all festivals he considered pagan.

Pierre de Coubertin of France spearheaded an effort in 1894 to revive the games, creating the International Olympic Committee which led to the first modern summer Olympics two years later in Athens, Greece. The IOC is considered the supreme organizational authority of the Olympic Games and is part of the Olympic Movement involving numerous international and national nonprofit amateur athlete organizations. From the outside, the Olympic system of developing rules, regulating them, and selecting athletes may seem simple. But Tug knew otherwise. Just like his previous jobs as an athletics director and commissioner, Tug recognized the multiple arms of responsibilities and relationships he needed to manage. If he thought keeping the American system running smoothly was a challenge, then ensuring the country was well represented in the field of international amateur sports was an even greater trial. Tangling even the smallest arm could have worldwide ramifications.

The making of an Olympian in America generally differs from most other countries because American amateur athletics are controlled by nonprofit organizations and funded privately. Consider the system or "feeder program" as a pyramid with a "very wide base leading to a very narrow tip for Olympians," said Rick Burton, a sports management professor at Syracuse University and a former USOC chief marketing officer. At the lowest level, anyone can play a sport. The pyramid narrows as the better players subsequently qualify for high school teams, college teams or clubs, then face tryouts for the Olympics. Ideally, the system extracts the best athletes in each sport to form the national team. The IOC recognizes the role of international sports federations or IFs—FIFA in soccer or ITF in tennis, for example—to establish rules for sports disciplines at the international level and to maintain the integrity of that sport. Countries may then have national Olympic committees such as the USOC in America and national governing bodies (NGB) for each sport—USA Swimming, for example. Created in 1894, the USOC is responsible for supporting, entering, and overseeing the US Olympic teams with the cooperation of NGBs, as well as the NCAA and the AAU, which feed collegiate and club athletes respectively into the system. "For Tug to have been the president of a national Olympic committee meant he had to put up with all the bureaucracy of not only the federations and the IOC above him, but of all the national governing bodies below him," Burton said. "Some of the federations are very well run and some are corrupt. Some are well established, and some have no money at all."[208] Although cooperation is a key factor in keeping the entire system running, that spirit hasn't always been at its best in America.

AAU vs NCAA

The Amateur Athletics Union (AAU), founded in 1888, was one of the first organizations created in the United States to promote and develop amateur sports and physical fitness programs. Organizers also recognized a great need to create common standards in amateur sports. When the USOC formed six years later, the AAU worked closely with that organization to select and prepare athletes for the Olympic Games. AAU programs provided most of the Olympic athletes until the NCAA came along. Eventually, the NCAA, high schools, colleges, and the military services soon produced most of the Olympic athletes. Although the number of AAU affiliated athletes was decreasing, that organization continued to maintain a dominant role in administering international competitions. That fact didn't sit

208 Personal interview via Zoom with Rick Burton and David B. Falk, Endowed Professor of Sport Management at Syracuse University, March 5, 2021.

well with NCAA officials who believed they should have more representatives on Olympic committees that made decisions concerning eligibility. Thus began a long-standing turf war over the "rights" of athletes in these programs—a dispute that hampered the US Olympic Movement. Occasionally, athletes sat out meets rather than risk suspension because of sanctioning issues. This meant some US participation in international competitions was either second best or nonexistent.[209]

Tug was all too familiar with the feud and its ramifications. During his tenure at Northwestern, the AAU refused to sanction a swimming meet between the Purple and the Chicago Athletic Association because Northwestern had competed in previous meets not sanctioned by the AAU. The meet was canceled, and Tug issued a statement declaring Northwestern did not recognize AAU as having "supreme control" over swimming and other sports. "In the future we will schedule our meets with colleges, universities and such clubs as are not subject to AAU control," Tug wrote.[210] In 1929, the Big Ten broke off relations with AAU, but the two groups later reached an agreement concerning the certification of college athletes. The USOC also changed its constitution giving greater voice to the colleges on the sports games committees.[211] "It was the first ray of sunshine in a long, bitter battle," Tug noted. "It was the first sign of any peaceful settlement."[212]

The forecast for the two organizations, however, remained cloudy, and in 1960 tempers flared again, forcing Tug to attempt a resolution. The NCAA council, tired of the growing number of complaints, voted not to respect AAU suspensions

209 Scannell, Nancy. 1978. "AAU–NCAA Conflict Nears Conclusion." Washingtonpost.com, June 25, 1978.
210 *The Big Ten*, 339-340.
211 Flath, Arnold. [1965] *A Summary of Relations Between the NCAA and AAU*, Proquest.
212 *The Big Ten*, 340.

unless both groups could agree on rules and procedures. The NCAA also canceled the Article of Alliance signed with the AAU in 1946. The split got little attention until *Sports Illustrated* published an article on September 25, 1961, discussing the controversy. Tug scheduled a joint meeting between leaders of the two groups hoping to mend the rift. Some sports writers believed if anyone could resolve the problems, it would be Tug. "Wilson is probably the very best peacemaker in the world of athletes," *Fort Worth Star-Telegram* columnist Flem Hall wrote. "He has established himself firmly with both college and non-college people as a man to be respected and trusted."[213] Hall's comments echoed accolades that had followed Tug throughout his career. Tug's deep voice and slow drawl exuded patience and tended to put people at ease, but he also was a smart, quick thinker who was firm in his beliefs.

Despite a prediction otherwise, Tug insisted he would not take sides in the argument and would work to find common ground. "But the one great thing must come from this meeting is that it doesn't matter who controls any vote," he told an Associated Press reporter, "but rather which group or combination of groups can come up with a program to train our youth for the Olympics."[214] Representatives from the NCAA and AAU met in Chicago on February 11–12, 1962, but failed to reach an agreement.[215] The ongoing feud would be left for someone else to try to resolve.

---

213 Hall, Flem. 1962, "The Sport Tide." *Fort Worth Star-Telegram*, January 26, 1962, 25.

214 Associated Press, *Johnson City Press* (Tennessee). 1962. "AAU-NCAA Peace Still In Question." February 2, 1962.

215 The feud wasn't put to rest until 1978 when legislators passed the Amateur Sports Act strengthening the USOC as the central coordinating agency of national amateur sports groups.

"Wilson is probably
the very best peacemaker
in the world of athletes."

Fort Worth Star-Telegram

Tug with Prince Philip, the Duke of Edinburgh

CHAPTER 16

Olympic Involvement from 1956 to 1964

Tug reportedly hadn't missed attending any of the world's greatest amateur athletic events, the Olympics, since he competed in 1920.[216]

1956 Olympics:
Melbourne, Australia

After participating for the next three decades as a spectator, Tug prepared to lead America's team into the Olympic stadium in Australia as the USOC president. Those preparations included fundraising—urging Americans to support their teams by reaching into their pocketbooks. He helped kickoff the Olympic fund drive in August 1955 during a dinner at the Indianapolis Athletic Club by lauding America's improvements in "athletic superiority." "America will not be ashamed of the team you will send to Melbourne," he said.[217]

Funding came from all types of sources. A sampling of donations show the range of support: school children gave

216 Cromie, Robert. 1956. "Wilson Lauds Olympic Squad." *Chicago Tribune*, October 30, 1956.
217 Eggert, Bill. 1955. "Wilson Helps Open Olympic Fund Drive." *The Indianapolis Star*, August 21, 1955, 53.

their pennies; national football fans contributed $360,000; clothing manufacturers outfitted the American athletes; and the Gillette company donated $160,000, collected ten cents at a time from every safety razor it sold during a two-month period.[218]

For the 1956 Summer Games, American athletes filled seven chartered planes—at a cost of $400,000—that transported them to Australia. Along the way, they stopped in Hawaii for thirty-six hours of rest. Tug told reporters the stopover was the "tonic"[219] athletes needed to put them in a winning mood. America was sending the "strongest team in history,"[220] he said as he confidently predicted its team would finish at the top.

It was an unusual year for the Olympics. Although the city of Melbourne played host to the Summer Games, the country's stringent quarantine laws forced officials to move the equestrian events to Stockholm, Sweden, in June. And since this was the first time the event was held in the Southern Hemisphere, the traditional Summer Games actually were in November and December to take advantage of some of Australia's warmest months. Athletes arrived in Melbourne to find store windows and streets decorated with Santa figures, colored lights, and fake snow for Christmas, with temperatures topping ninety-five degrees on some days.

Political strife offered yet another contradiction. At least seven countries either boycotted the games or pulled out at the last minute because of conflicts with other countries. Egypt, Iraq, and Lebanon boycotted the games because of the Suez Crisis. The Netherlands, Spain, and Switzerland pulled out because of disagreements with the Soviet Union, and the

218 Cromie, Robert. 1956. "Wilson Lauds Olympic Squad." *Chicago Tribune*, October 30, 1956.
219 Associated Press *Fort Worth Star-Telegram* (Fort Worth, Texas), 1956. "U.S. Team Rests." November 7, 1956, 31.
220 Associated Press *Racine Journal-Times*. 1956. "What's Ahead in 1956." January 1, 1956, 3.

People's Republic of China refused to send athletes because the Republic of China was participating. Even a water polo match between Hungary and the Soviet Union turned into a bloodbath fueled by Cold War tensions. All this dissension occurred despite the event being billed as the "Friendly Games." East and West Germany, however, put aside their differences to compete as one team.

Entering the stadium just behind the USA placard and American flag must have brought back a lot of wonderful memories for Tug as he helped lead 297 American athletes around the track in front of an estimated 180,000 sports fans. Groups of athletes stood at attention in the infield as Prince Philip, the Duke of Edinburgh, declared the games to be open.

The highlight of the games for the American team came from sprinter Bobby Morrow who earned three gold medals while his hero, Jesse Owens, watched from the stands. Owens had won four gold medals in the 1936 Olympic Games in Berlin, Germany. The United States finished the Melbourne Games with seventy-four total medals, including thirty-two gold. But much to Tug's chagrin, the Soviet Union won the games with ninety-eight total medals, of which thirty-seven were gold.

1960 Olympics:
Rome, Italy

Italy played host to the summer Olympics for the first time in 1960, having missed an opportunity in 1908 when the eruption of Mount Vesuvius forced a moved to London.[221] Although participants may not have realized it at the time, the Summer Olympics in Rome, Italy, represented another turning point in the history of the games. In retrospect, these games were "the end of something or the start of something,"

---

221 Although the eruption came two years before the official games, concerned Olympic officials selected another city.

journalist David Maraniss later noted. Competition involved much more than just strength, agility, and fair play. Issues of race, gender, and Cold War politics also played roles as if they were the harbinger of worldwide change. "Life was changing noticeably during those final months of 1960; the world seemed on the cusp not just of a new decade but of a new cultural era. No one could say precisely what the future would bring, but some hints, good and bad, could be gleaned from the Olympics in Rome," Maraniss wrote.[222] It was, as *Philadelphia Inquirer* sports columnist Bob Ford put it, "17 days that defined the modern world."

Black athletes took on more prominent roles and garnered more media attention during these Games. Long-distance runner Abebe Bikila of Ethiopia ran the marathon barefoot, earning the first gold medal won by a Black African. He would repeat his performance in 1964, but this time with his shoes on. Texan Rafer Johnson became the first Black American athlete to carry the US flag during opening ceremonies. He later won the gold medal in the decathlon. Boxer Cassius Clay (later changed his name to Muhammad Ali) of Kentucky also won a gold, jump-starting a professional career that earned him the title "The Greatest." And former polio patient, Wilma Rudolph, won three gold medals in sprint events—a performance that earned the Black Tennessee native the title of "The Fastest Woman in the World." Their performances, however, exposed the hypocrisy of American social attitudes. While honoring Johnson, Clay, and Rudolph for their accomplishments, these athletes were barred from eating in many American restaurants because of the color of their skin.

Racial equality also was an issue in South Africa. Olympic officials considered barring that country from sending a team unless it included Black athletes. South African officials,

---

222 Maraniss, David. 2008. *Rome 1960: The Olympics That Changed the World.* New York, NY, Simon & Schuster, 2008, 4515 (Kindle).

however, argued there were no Black athletes good enough to compete[223] at that level. Brundage contended the threat against South Africa crossed the line into politics by punishing athletes for the policies of a government.

Politics caused problems involving German and Chinese athletes. Continued political division between the German Democratic Republic (East Germany) and Federal Republic of Germany (West Germany) left in question whether the country's athletes would again compete as one team or two. They appeared together as the United Team of Germany (EUA), but back home fans kept score concerning whether East or West athletes did best. However, that wasn't the resolution for a dispute between the People's Republic of China (PRC) and the Republic of China (ROC) or Taiwan. The ROC team was forced to compete under the name of Formosa (the name for the island) because of objections from mainland China authorities—an unpopular decision for team members who marched behind a sign reading "UNDER PROTEST" during the parade of nations.

The 1960 Summer Olympics saw a record 611 women athletes competing in twenty-nine events—up from 376 women competitors in twenty-six events in Italy four years earlier. The number of female athletes continued to rise in subsequent Olympiads once IOC officials began relaxing restrictions against women. The prevailing attitude that women were too delicate or that it was unladylike to compete in certain athletic events—long-distance running, for example—previously had stymied female athletics. Young women, like sixteen-year-old Chris von Saltza of the United States, also proved age did not bind athleticism. She won three golds and one silver in swimming. These Olympics also marked the use of the fiberglass pole that changed vaulting from a

---

223 South Africa was banned after the 1960 Olympics due to its policy of apartheid. The country repealed the policy and returned to Olympic competition in 1992.

sport of power to one of agility; and it marked the birth of a system to test athletes for banned substances after evidence showed amphetamines may have played a role in the death of a Danish cyclist who crashed and died while competing.[224]

The Rome Olympics was the first to be fully covered by television and to be televised in North America. It wasn't easy, though. CBS paid $394,000 for exclusive rights to broadcast in the United States, but without the access to satellites, getting the film back across the Atlantic Ocean required a relay race of a different kind. Filmed events were edited in Rome and then fed to a Paris location where it was recorded onto compatible tapes and sent on jet planes to New York City where broadcasts highlighted the events the same day as the events occurred. The daily broadcast by Jim McKay launched his career as a sports journalist, which included covering twelve Olympic Games and playing the host of ABC's popular "Wide World of Sports."

For Tug, walking into an Olympic stadium as part of the US delegation never became a routine part of his role as USOC president. Every time seemed like it was his first. He wasn't just witnessing history; he was a part of it.

The day before opening ceremonies in Rome, Tug watched as Pope John XXIII blessed nearly five thousand athletes gathered at St. Peter's Square in a ceremony replete with the regal sound of Italian trombas and peeling church bells. During the opening ceremony, Tug marched in step with the group of American athletes, all dressed in matching white pants, blue blazers, and white hats with patriotic colored bands. They watched and listened as a hymn composed by Spiros Samaras made its debut as the official Olympic anthem while the games' traditional five-ring flag was raised.

---

224 Knud Enemark Jensen suffered a heat stroke during 108-degree temperatures. He crashed and fractured his skull, but reportedly during an autopsy there were amphetamines found in his system, raising questions on whether drugs may have affected his performance that day.

Tug, second from right, helps lead American athletes in the traditional Olympic Parade of Nations in 1964.

Tug addressed the final outcomes in speeches to social groups around the US after returning home. "The Olympic Games are no longer just a track meet," he told a group at the Byline Club in Kansas City.[225] He had bragged before that America was sending its best team ever to Rome, but the final results offered a mixed bag of success. Rudolph, Clay, and others recorded amazing victories, but American gymnasts had been shut out of medal contention, and nine American world champions had failed to make the finals. US athletes won 71 medals, including 34 gold, but finished second to the Russians again, who collected 103 total medals including 43 gold. "We did as well as we could," Kansas University coach Bill Easton, who sent five Jayhawk athletes to Rome, told the group. "The competition is getting fiercer all the time. Tokyo will be even bigger, better and tougher and we must produce a team capable of facing the world."[226]

---

225 Busby, Bob. 1960. "Wilson Calls for Accent on Athletics." *The Kansas City Times*, September 27, 1960, 13.
226 Busby, Bob. 1960. "Wilson Calls for Accent on Athletics." *The Kansas City Times*, September 27, 1960, 13.

1964 Olympics:
Tokyo, Japan

The turf war between the AAU and NCAA reared its ugly head again in early 1963 when AAU's executive director, Colonel Don Hull, claimed Tug and USOC secretary Asa Bushnell violated the rules when they endorsed the NCAA-backed federations. Rule twenty-four of the International Olympic Committee requires national Olympic committees to cooperate with national bodies affiliated with the international body, but that affiliate must be the one recognized by the IOC. The AAU, Hull noted, is the recognized affiliate for track and field.

The renewed dispute came to a head later that year at the National AAU Track Championship in St. Louis. Some collegiate standouts, including runner Bob Hayes of Florida A&M, threatened to boycott the event until an arbitrator stepped in. The championships were integral to forming a team invited to compete in a Russian meet, but both organizations were still debating who had the authority to decide team members. The arbitrator, appointed by President Dwight D. Eisenhower, was none other than General Douglas MacArthur. MacArthur was familiar with the dispute between the two groups, considering he had previously served as USOC president.[227] Tug declined to intervene because the Olympic Committee would not be active until the next year. Still, Tug expressed deep concern about the dispute's potential effect on America's reputation. "The most unfortunate aspect of the dispute . . . and this is something which neither can deny . . . is that we have given the entire world a poor picture of us," he said.[228] Although convinced the US would send its strongest possible team to Russia, Tug said future invitations

---

227 Served as president during the 1928 Olympics in Amsterdam. He was in his early 80s when Eisenhower called upon him to arbitrate the AAU-NCAA dispute.
228 Devine, Tommy. 1963. "Olympic Leader Middle Man in Power Struggle." *The Miami News*, July 19, 1963.

to foreign competitions may be jeopardized if the continued dispute meant the United States could not send its top stars. "I would much rather decline a bid than be represented by athletes who admittedly are not our best," he said.[229]

Tug told *Miami News* reporter Tommy Devine that trying to resolve the struggle for control "is the most difficult and involved in his career." Despite his efforts to be impartial, Tug said he had been seen as supporting colleges because of his experience as an athletic director and Big Ten commissioner. He suggested the issue may need to be reviewed by fresh eyes. "Sometimes I feel that I, and the other people who have been controversial figures on the Olympics, collegiate or AAU side, might promote a speedier settlement if we stepped aside," he said.[230] Tug, whose term was about to end, told Devine he hadn't decided whether he would accept another nomination if it was offered.

The Japanese had something to prove to the world in 1964. Tokyo had been selected as the host city for the 1940 Olympics, but the honor passed to Helsinki, Finland, because of Japan's invasion of China.[231] The Olympics were later canceled because of the outbreak of World War II. Allied forces, led by the United States, occupied Japan for seven years after the Japanese lost the war. Just a dozen years later, the Japanese were eager to show their progress and desire to reemerge onto the world stage as being peaceful and economically confident.[232] It would be the first time the Olympics would be conducted in Asia. Unlike hosts in previous Olympiads, the Japanese offered a more

---

229 Devine, Tommy. 1963. "Olympic Leader Middle Man in Power Struggle." *The Miami News,* July 10, 1963, 9.
230 Devine, Tommy. 1963. "Olympic Leader Middle Man in Power Struggle." *The Miami News,* July 10, 1963, 9.
231 Tokyo, Japan, also was selected for the 2020 Olympics, which were postponed for one year due to a pandemic.
232 Martin, Alexander. 2013. "The 1964 Olympics: A Turning Point for Japan." September 5, 2013, wsj.com.

entertaining opening ceremony, including the release of hundreds of balloons and a skywriting airplane that recreated the interlocking Olympic rings with smoke. Cannon shots boomed as the athletic teams—including Americans wearing cowboy hats—marched into the stadium filled to capacity with 85,000 spectators. The Olympic torch was lit by Yoshinori Sakai, an athlete born on August 6, 1945, the day American forces dropped the atomic bomb on Hiroshima. Sakai was specifically selected for the task as a symbol of the country's rebirth. The Tokyo Olympics were the first to be broadcast live to every continent via satellite. In Japan, over two million tickets were sold, but the broadcasts brought in another six hundred to eight hundred million viewers worldwide.

Bob Hayes, who had previously threatened to boycott a qualifying meet, made the Olympic team and finished with two gold medals in running events.[233] Other notable gold-medal performances included boxer Joe Frazier, who became the first professional boxer to defeat Muhammad Ali; eighteen-year-old swimmer Don Schollander, who became the first American to win four golds in a single Olympics; and fifteen-year-old Sharon Stouder, who won three golds and one silver in swimming events.

Underdog Billy Mills shocked the world with an Olympic gold run in the 10,000 meters. The win marked one of the biggest upsets in Olympic history. Teammate Robert "Bob" Schul also pulled off an unexpected win—coming from behind on a muddy track to win gold in the 5,000-meter race. In an interview with a United Press International reporter, Tug contended the wins by Mills and Schul were the start of a "new era" for long-distance running in America—potentially inspiring young athletes to take up the sport. "There is just no limit to what it is going to do for long-distance running back

---

233 After the Olympics, Hayes played professional football and was on the Dallas Cowboys team when it won the Super Bowl in 1970. Hayes is the only athlete to have ever earned an Olympic gold and a Super Bowl title.

home," he said. "Mills and Schul proved that long-distance running can be glamorous."[234]

Tug was elated with the final overall results. US athletes took home ninety medals, including thirty-six gold, to edge out the Soviet Union in the medal count. Although the Russians had won six more medals than the US, their gold count ended at thirty. In the Olympics, the number of gold medals earned is more important than the total amount of medals won. The Japanese ended the games with an impressive showing of twenty-nine medals, including sixteen gold, finishing in third place. Tug couldn't offer enough praise for the host. "Things could not have been more perfect from our standpoint," he said. "I don't see how any city will surpass the Tokyo games."[235]

234 United Press International, *The Monitor* (McAllen, Texas). 1963. "U.S. Olympic Head Predicts Good Era." October 26, 1963, 8.
235 United Press International, The Monitor (McAllen, Texas). 1963. "U.S. Olympic Head Predicts Good Era." October 26, 1963, 8.

Tug Wilson at the 1955 Pan American
Games in Mexico City. This photo was given
to Tug by Bill Armstrong, chairman of the
National AAU Public Relations Committee.

CHAPTER 17

Building Stronger American Olympians

The Olympics' official motto "Citius, Altius, Fortius,"— Latin for "Faster, Higher, Stronger"—reflects the goal for athletic competitors worldwide, striving to be the best not just as an individual, but as a country as well. For individual athletes, winning an Olympic medal or several medals is comparable to being the best of the best. But is it the same for a country as a whole? Does winning the most medals have any significance outside the world of athletics?

Tug may not have been willing to admit it, but his own words suggest his focus on "beating the Russians" was just as important in other realms. The medal count—tracked intensely by the media—generally determines the overall winner, although under the IOC system the number of gold medals "count" more than the overall number. Under that system, the United States may place second overall even if its athletes garnered the most medals but had fewer gold.

Tug's tenure as USOC president overlapped with the Cold War era—a period of tension over ideological differences between the United States and the Soviet Union. In Russia and China, amateur sports fell under a governmental entity, such as a ministry of sports. Athletes are selected at a young age and receive training and schooling by a government-funded agency. Purists argued that this constitutes a professional athlete, and therefore this person should be ineligible to compete in the Olympics. For decades, the debate centered on what defines a professional and whether professionals should be allowed.[236] For officials on both sides, coming out on top reflected not only the best team, but the best country athletically, politically, or otherwise. "Winning an Olympic medal or beating a Soviet track team have become almost as important a factor in the 'cold war' as putting a man on the moon," according to an Associated Press report.[237]

Tug analyzed previous Olympic outcomes, such as a college coach reviewing game tapes, and often touted America's "superiority" in amateur sports during speeches and media interviews throughout the country. His confidence in Olympic athletes was unshakable. The Olympic squad in 1956 was the "finest in our history." In 1960, it was "the greatest Olympic team we have ever fielded." And in 1964, "We are ready with the best team we ever have had at an Olympiad." Statistics don't lie. As of 2020, America has earned more medals by far in the Summer Olympics than any other country—2,636 in all—but when considering the average number of medals from Summer Games attended, the Soviet Union ranks first with an average of 112 medals compared with a 94 average by the US.[238]

---

236 In 1986, the International Federation opened the Olympics to professional athletes.
237 Associated Press, *The Journal-Times* (Racine, Wisconsin). 1962. "AAU, NCAA Must End Trouble or Uncle Sam Will Intervene." February 4, 1962, 29.
238 "All-Time Olympic Games Medal Tally (Summer Olympics)," topendsports. com. The Soviet Union didn't attend the same number of Olympics as the United States, so an average developed by topendsports.com offers an arguably better perspective of the medal race. The stats take into consideration the breakup of the Soviet Union.

Success Is Relative

Success in the Olympics is relative. For some countries, just sending a team to compete is a success. For others, the bar is a little higher. Consider marathoner Abebe Bikila who was hailed a hero for bringing home the only medals—both gold—from the 1960 and 1964 Olympics representing Ethiopia. They awarded Bikila Order of the Star of Ethiopia, promoted him in rank in the Imperial Guard, and gave him access to a chauffeured-driven vehicle for bringing honor to the country. But for the world superpowers, the Olympics and the medal count seemed extremely important to how the rest of the world viewed them. In his book *Rome 1960* journalist David Maraniss offered evidence of the US and the Russia using the Olympics in a propaganda campaign. "If the Games were a front in the propaganda battle of the cold war, the Soviets could claim victory," he said.[239]

Improving the American Athletic Program from the Roots Up

Countries tend to dominate sports that originated in their country. America, for example, has never failed to medal in basketball, a game invented in 1891 in Massachusetts. Out of eighteen Olympic appearances, the US basketball team has won fifteen gold medals. Tug believed America lagged in what he considered minor sports such as shooting, canoeing, gymnastics, cycling, and fencing. "No country in the world should be as good with guns as we should be," he told a *Chicago Tribune* reporter. "After all our country was founded on shooting." He cited the lack of training facilities as the cause. "We're poor at it because we only have two ranges in the country," he said, noting that shooting ranges in Fort Benny,

---

239 Maraniss, David. 2008. *Rome 1960: The Olympics That Changed the World.* New York, NY, Simon & Schuster, 2008, 5553 (Kindle).

Georgia, and Waukegan, Illinois, were the only ones that had the required 400-yard-long range.[240]

The 1964 winter Olympics in Austria offers another example. The US finished eighth with seven total medals, only one of which was gold. "Our poor showing in the Winter Olympics shouldn't have surprised anybody," Tug said, "since we are not really a winter sports country."[241] The catastrophic loss of the entire US skating team in a 1961 plane crash,[242] also was a likely contributing factor.

Journalist Maraniss proposed the "stirring" in the political hierarchy worldwide during the 1960s, included athletics. He noted nations that didn't exist prior to the Melbourne Games competed in Rome with distinction. "The US scares not a soul anymore," he wrote. "Once the Americans dominated the show. They don't anymore, nor are they likely to do so again."[243]

Tug recognized tremendous improvements in American athletes during the late 1950s and early 1960s. "We haven't reached our peak yet. We're still getting better all the time, not only in the so-called major sports, but also in the minor sports." He repeatedly touted a focus on finding and developing athletes in order to remain competitive and to build a stronger program. "For decades our Olympic program consisted simply of raising money, then conducting trials, then taking the kids overseas and back again. Then the whole thing would be forgotten for another four years," Tug told the *Chicago Tribune*. "But now we have realized, I think, that we have to get down to the grassroots and develop the kids and instill Olympic ideas in their hearts."[244] Getting down to the grassroots meant supporting programs at

---

240 *Chicago Tribune*. 1964. "In the Wake of the News." April 1, 1964, 53.
241 *Chicago Tribune*. 1964. "In the Wake of the News." April 1, 1964, 53.
242 Eighteen US skaters and sixteen people accompanying them to the World Figure Skating Championships in Czechoslovakia died when their plane crashed on February 15, 1961, in Belgium.
243 Maraniss, David, 2008. *Rome 1960: The Olympics That Changed the World*. New York, NY. Simon & Schuster, 2008, 5568 (Kindle).
244 *Chicago Tribune*. 1964. "In the Wake of the News." April 1, 1964, 53.

the YMCA in high schools, and in other places, such as police departments across the country that were conducting judo classes for children.

He especially endorsed recruiting more female athletes, noting that America lagged in that area. "Physical education teachers who have never looked with great pleasure on competition by girls, are finally starting to change their minds," he said. "We've got to go to the high schools, into the cities and clubs, to encourage boys and girls who have ability. They must have the finest coaches, good equipment and suitable competition." He also called for American athletes to compete in more international events. "It doesn't do our teams any good to beat one another," he said. "We need to bring teams in that are better than we are or go to them."[245]

The urgency to build a stronger Olympic team even hit home with President Kennedy, who within six months of taking office, turned attention to the issue of physical fitness. He appointed Charles "Bob" Wilkinson as a special consultant to the president on the issue to help promote sports participation and physical fitness.[246]

The feud over track and field spilled over into 1965, prompting more governmental attempts to resolve the issue once and for all. Robert Kennedy, a Democrat from New York, testified before the Senate Commerce Committee, proposing a plan that included giving the USOC broader powers to impose binding arbitration. Kennedy, however, wasn't optimistic any agreement reached between the two factions would ever hold. As US Attorney General, Robert Kennedy had twice before helped negotiate an agreement only to see relationships fall apart again. He suggested that creating a national sports foundation may be the answer. Tug told committee members he supported Robert Kennedy's plan.[247]

---

245 *Chicago Tribune*. 1964. "In the Wake of the News." April 1, 1964, 53.
246 Maraniss, David, 2008. *Rome 1960: The Olympics That Changed the World*. New York, NY. Simon & Schuster, 2008, 5606 (Kindle).
247 *Asbury Park Press*, Associated Press. 1965. "R.F. Kennedy's Plan Supported." August 27, 1965.

Five months before Tug's term as USOC president was set to expire, its executive committee announced a "major shake-up" within the organization. "Wilson Out as Olympic President," the *Capital Times* in Madison, Wisconsin, declared. The committee had recommended a whole new slate of officers, including Douglas F. Roby of Detroit as president. Roby had served as the USOC's vice president under Tug and was a past president of the AAU. "The committee felt it was in the best interest of the Olympic movement and in order to create a new image and new interest that a rotation of officers be made," an unnamed spokesperson said.[248] That certainly was news to Tug, who issued a mild rebuke. "I think I got a bum rap," he said in an article published in *The Minnesota Star*. Tug said he had previously told the nominating committee he would not consider another term. "Despite that, the publicity that was sent out indicated that I had been thrown out," he said. "Such treatment doesn't make one feel too good after giving as much as I have for so many years without a single penny of pay."[249] Despite the awkward ending to his tenure, Tug left the organization with the honorary title of "USOC President Emeritus."

248 *The Capital Times* (Madison, Wisconsin). 1965. "Wilson Out as Olympic President." July 26, 1965, 12.
249 The article "Lowdown on Sports," written by Charles Johnson and published in *The Minneapolis Star* on August 5, 1965, embarrassed Tug Wilson.

"Now we have realized,
I think, that we have to
get down to the grassroots
and develop the kids and
instill Olympic ideas
in their hearts."

Tug Wilson

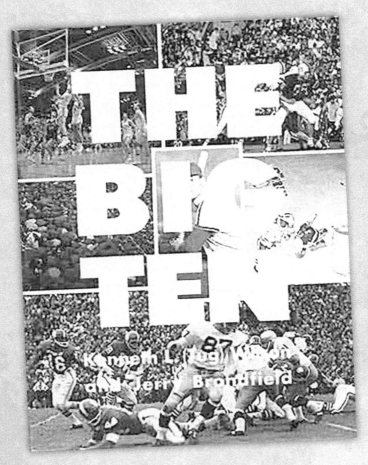

Cover of *The Big Ten* book

CHAPTER 18

The Golden Years

Tug retired in 1965, but he wasn't done with his life's work just yet. He wasted no time is starting to work on another project he had pondered for some time—a book chronicling the year-to-year history of the Big Ten. He joined forces with Jerry Brondfield, a sports journalist and editor with Scholastic Inc., to produce what a New Jersey reporter described as a "monument to nostalgia."[250] Released in 1967, *The Big Ten* consisted of nearly five hundred pages of statistics, short biographies on star players and coaches, photographs, and Tug's own story. Sports writers across the country recommended the book for true sports fans, although one Indiana columnist noted that the $14.95 price tag was too costly for the average person.[251] The *Chicago Tribune* even ran excerpts from the book in a weekly column under Tug's and Brondfield's bylines.

Tug continued to accept speaking engagements and even attended the 1968 Olympics in Mexico—games made memorable by two African-American athletes who each

---

250 Howat, Mark. 1967. "Football and Other Sports." *The Record* (Hackensack, New Jersey), December 2, 1967.
251 Doyle, Joe. 1967. "According to Doyle." *The South Bend Tribune,* October 19, 1967.

Tug with his brother, Henry, during the Atwood
centennial in 1973 (Atwood Herald photo)

raised a black-gloved fist in protest during the playing of the
US national anthem.[252]

What likely was Tug's last visit to Atwood came in
1973 when he and his brother, Henry, attended the town's
centennial celebration. The seventy-seven-year-old Tug
participated in a parade down Main Street.

In his final years, Tug and Dorothy[253] lived in Wilmette,
Illinois, about fourteen miles north of downtown Chicago.
Tug was especially proud of his daughters' choices of schools
to continue their education. Suzanne studied at Michigan
before transferring to Northwestern to finish her degree

---

252 Runners Tommie Smith and John Carlos lifted their fists while on the
podium as a gesture for human rights.
253 Dorothy Wilson died in 1981 and is buried next to her husband in Lexington.

in education.[254] Nancy earned her bachelor's degree at the University of Illinois and a master's degree in journalism from Northwestern.[255] "We were truly a Big Ten family," Tug wrote.[256]

Tug and his wife celebrated their fifty-fifth wedding anniversary in January 1979; about a month later, Tug died at Presbyterian Hospital in Evanston at the age of eighty-two. His ashes were buried in Lexington, his wife's hometown. His death was announced in a brief article in the *New York Times,* and in the following months, sports journalists all over the country eulogized Tug in personal columns dedicated to "the country's most influential person in amateur sports."[257] They told a story of a humble, honest man who performed his duties with dignity and who loved to reminisce about the past.

During his tenure as USOC president, American athletes brought home ninety-two gold medals—eighty-six from the summer events and six in the winter events. Tug, himself, defied the odds to become an Olympic athlete, who was thrilled with just having the opportunity to compete, and in the end, he received in words what he didn't bring home from Antwerp.

As journalist David Condon wrote, Tug was a "gold medal man."

---

254 Suzanne taught kindergarten at Evanston Elementary School for nineteen years before dying in 1984 at the age of fifty.

255 Nancy married Donald M. Kellough, and together they had three children: Linda, Douglas(a.k.a. "Tug"), and Donald. She died in 2009 at the age of seventy-eight.

256 *The Big Ten*, 152.

257 Condon, David. 1979. "Tug Wilson Always Performed as Gold Medal Winner." *Chicago Tribune,* February 6, 1979.

EPILOGUE

There is nothing my grandfather enjoyed more than telling a good story, and with his deep voice and rumbling laugh, he was a master storyteller. How he would have enjoyed this biography and would probably have added a few extra details, punctuated with jabs of his smoldering stogie. Tales of his boyhood on a downstate Illinois farm were his favorite. Our family loves the image of him cracking up the actor Charlton Heston (known for his portrayal of Ben-Hur driving a wild Roman chariot) with stories of hanging onto a runaway mule-drawn farm wagon.

This book has given our family the opportunity to rediscover our grandfather and the full range of his experience and accomplishments. Visiting Atwood, meeting people who remember him and his family, and participating in the town's commemoration events have been unexpectedly moving. Atwood's dedication and enthusiasm for honoring him has touched our family.

Growing up in a community like Atwood truly shaped Tug Wilson's values and ability to move easily in the larger world. Yet he remained connected to his hometown, and for both him and our grandmother, who also grew up in a small Illinois farm town, their friends from central Illinois were the ones closest to their hearts.

Tug Wilson was a staunch believer in the value of truly amateur athletics and its ability to develop physical health and good character, a conviction born of his own experience. He remained grateful throughout his life for the world of opportunity opened to him and his family by competitive sports.

Throughout his career, he always took the time to sincerely acknowledge those mentors who saw more potential in him than he perhaps saw in himself and who always urged him to take the next step. This biography provides an opportunity to acknowledge and appreciate Tug Wilson's contributions to the world of amateur athletics, all beginning with a daily run after farm chores from his home to a schoolhouse near Atwood, Illinois.

Linda Kellough
September 2021

Vanessa E. Curry's journalism career spans nearly thirty-five years and includes experience as an award-winning writer, photographer, editor, and college instructor. She earned a bachelor of science degree in mass communication and a master's degree in interdisciplinary studies with emphasis on journalism, political science, and criminal justice. She enjoys researching and writing about legal and social issues, as well as history.

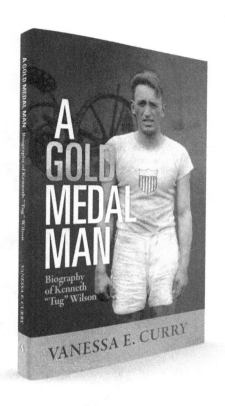

FOR MORE AUTHOR INFORMATION AND TO
ORDER BOOKS IN BULK, PLEASE VISIT:
VANESSACURRY.COM

OR SEND AN EMAIL TO
VANESSA_CURRY@ATT.NET

CPSIA information can be obtained
at www.ICGtesting.com
Printed in the USA
LVHW111939210722
723810LV00001B/3

9 781953 555298